DISCOVERY

DISCOVERY
THE BAD COMPANY™ BOOK SIX

CRAIG MARTELLE

MICHAEL ANDERLE

LMBPN Publishing
PMB 196, 2540 South Maryland Pkwy
Las Vegas, NV 89109

First US edition, May 2019
ebook ISBN: 978-1-64202-232-2
Print ISBN: 978-1-64202-705-1

We can't write without those who support us
On the home front, we thank you for being there for us

We wouldn't be able to do this for a living if it weren't for our readers
We thank you for reading our books

DISCOVERY TEAM

Thanks to our Beta Readers

Micky Cocker, Dr. Jim Caplan, Kelly O'Donnell, and John Ashmore

Thanks to the JIT Readers

Jeff Goode
Nicole Emens
Dorothy Lloyd
Kelly O'Donnell
Daniel Weigert
Diane L. Smith
James Caplan
Peter Manis
Micky Cocker
Jeff Eaton
Robert Brooks
Misty Roa
John Ashmore
Paul Westman

If I've missed anyone, please let me know!

Editor
Lynne Stiegler

CHARACTERS & TIMELINE

World's Worst Day Ever (WWDE)

WWDE + 20 years, Terry Henry returns from self-imposed exile. The Terry Henry Walton Chronicles detail his adventures from that time to WWDE+150

WWDE + 150 years – Michael returns to Earth. BA returns to Earth. TH & Char go to space

Key Players

- Terry Henry Walton (was forty-five on the WWDE)—called TH by his friends. Enhanced with nanocytes by Bethany Anne herself (Queen of High Tortuga after Federation is formed and Empire is dissolved), wears the rank of colonel, lead the Force de Guerre (FDG), a military unit that he established on WWDE+20 years, and now leads the Bad Company's Direct Action Branch.

- Charumati (was sixty-five on the WWDE)—A werewolf, married to Terry, carries the rank of major but is his equal partner
- Kimber (born WWDE+15 years, adopted approximately WWDE+25 years by TH & Char, enhanced on WWDE+65 years)—Major
- Her husband Auburn Weathers (enhanced on WWDE+82 years)—provides logistics support
- Kaeden (born WWDE+16 years, adopted approximately WWDE+24 years by TH & Char, enhanced on WWDE+65 years) – a major
- His wife Marcie Spires (born on WWDE+22 years, naturally enhanced)—Colonel
- Cory (born WWDE+25 years, naturally enhanced, gifted with the power to heal)
- Her husband Ramses—Major, died on Benitus Seven, WWDE+153 years
- Kailin, Auburn & Kimber's son (born on WWDE+78 years)

Vampires

- Joseph (born three hundred years before the WWDE)
- Petricia (born WWDE+30 years)

Pricolici (Werewolves that walk upright)

- Nathan Lowell (President of the Bad Company and Bethany Anne's Chief of Intelligence)
- Ecaterina (Nathan's spouse)
- Christina (Nathan & Ecaterina's daughter)

Werewolves

- Sue & Timmons (long-term members of Char's pack)
- Shonna & Merrit (long-term members of Char's pack)
- Ted (with Felicity, an enhanced human)

Weretigers born before the WWDE:

- Aaron & Yanmei

Humans (enhanced)

- Micky San Marino, Captain of the *War Axe*
- Commander Suresha, *War Axe* Department Head – Engines
- Commander MacEachthighearna (Mac), *War Axe* Department Head—Environmental
- Commander Blagun Lagunov, *War Axe* Department—Structure
- Commander Oscar Wirth, *War Axe* Department Head—Stores
- Lieutenant Clodagh Shortall, *War Axe* engine technician

- Sergeant Fitzroy, a martial arts expert and platoon sergeant
- Kelly, Capples, Fleeter, Praeter, & Duncan—mech drivers

<u>Other Key Characters</u>

- Dokken (a sentient German Shepherd)
- Floyd (a sentient and sweet wombat who gives gifts of poop cubes when she loves you)
- The Good King Wenceslaus (an orange tabby domestic cat who thinks he's a weretiger, all fifteen pounds of him)
- K'Thrall—a four-legged Yollin, used to be systems analyst on the *War Axe,* a warrior with the Bad Company
- Ruzfell – new systems specialist on the *War Axe*
- Clifton—human pilot of the *War Axe*
- Bundin—a four-legged shell-backed blue stalk-headed alien from Poddern
- Ankh'Po'Turn—a small bald humanoid from Crenellia. Erasmus, one of Plato's Stepchildren, is his AI
- General Smedley Butler – EI/AI on the *War Axe,* who they call The General
- Plato – Ted's AI from R&D
- Dionysus – the AI tasked to assist with running Keeg Station
- Iracitus – the AI assisting Shonna & Merrit in the asteroid mining effort

- Paithoon – A Belzonian, escort for Kaeden & Marcie
- Bon Tap – a teal-skinned, silver-haired Malatian, a warrior in the Bad Company
- Slikira – an Ixtali, four legs, a spider race, called "Slicker," a warrior in the Bad Company

Other Bad Company warriors: Tim, "Skates" Mardigan, Chris Bo Runner (Harborian), Jones, Einar, Gefelton, Eldis (wife is Xianna, a green-skinned Torregidoran female), B'Ichi Aharche (Keome)

CHAPTER ONE

<u>Venus Pleasure Moon orbiting Cygnus VI</u>

"Y'all have fun now, ya hear," Felicity drawled.

Terry smirked, but Charumati, the purple-eyed werewolf, delivered a beaming smile. "There's no doubt about that. He left his comm on the *War Axe*."

"No untimely calls to interrupt the good stuff. We have to go; the kids are expecting us." Felicity waved from the open hatch and went inside *Ramses' Chariot*, a smallish frigate that Ted had acquired for his personal use in support of the Etheric Federation.

Ted hadn't said goodbye. He had been working on breaking the alien engineering for their cloak. He was close, and no one was going to interfere. Except for Felicity. She was the only person in the universe who could get inside his Asperger-armored emotional shields. It didn't mean he didn't care, it only meant he was busy. Char was his alpha, and he would do as he was told, but there was no need to push him. He was doing what she needed him to do: support the Bad Company.

Werewolves had a separate chain of command, despite Terry's Marine Corps adherence to good order and discipline. He had softened his stance over time because on the matter of being the pack's alpha, Char was unyielding. Terry's life had been saved by Bethany Anne because of his sacrifices in the name of Justice. She had introduced his battered and frozen body to the Pod-doc for a process that installed nanocytes to become one with him, drawing power from the Etheric to make his body stronger, heal his wounds, and keep his cells fresh. The process had also prolonged his life.

In the beginning, the Queen told him it would give an extra hundred years, time she challenged him to use in making a difference for humanity. That had been over one hundred and fifty years ago. Terry and Char had married a while after that, and their nanocytes had melded to make the couple greater than their individual parts. No one knew if they would ever age.

A werewolf with a boosted spouse who wasn't a Were. Same situation as Felicity and Ted, but in the latter case, the individual's nanos didn't feed off each other to grow into something more. Terry and Char were unique. And they still did the Queen's bidding, and would, no matter how long they lived.

The runabout lifted off and accelerated toward space, staying outside the traffic lanes because it refused to be so constrained.

Just like Terry and Char. Their vacation adventure had just begun.

Once the ship was gone, Terry hoisted their one bag onto his shoulder, and together, they walked toward check-in. They hadn't brought much. Char had insisted on no technology.

Terry was good with that. Vacation. Exploring and resting. Enjoying each other's company, as they had for the previous hundred and fifty years.

Yet they still acted like newlyweds who were also best friends. And Char still never knew what Terry would say next.

"I wish I would have spent more time with Bethany Anne," Terry began.

Char looked askance at her husband. "After the bowing and scraping, I'm surprised she let you spend any time at all with her."

"She was the Queen, then the Empress, and now the Queen again. How am I supposed to keep up with her exaltedness?"

"By treating her like a normal human being." Char chuckled. "Maybe you should acquire a greater appreciation for women's shoes."

Terry's mouth worked, but he couldn't generate the words. He stopped trying. "I got nothing."

"And *that's* why you didn't spend more time with BA."

"Maybe you could punch me in the face. It would hurt less." Terry looked to see if he had gotten a rise out of his wife, but she shrugged. Water off a duck's back.

The entryway to the resort was a glorious affair. Magnificent iridescent arches with fountains sent multicolored waves over the guests, creating a living tunnel through which they walked to get to registration.

But the concierge caught them before they reached the desk.

"My! Don't you two look like the epitome of health and vigor?"

Terry's skin crawled. He had loathed the sales pitches before the World's Worst Day Ever and hadn't missed them when they were gone. Welcome to the universe! Hucksters and town criers were on the rebound.

Terry tried to brush past the man, but he offered a delicate string of flowers to Char. "You should wear these around your neck for luck."

She paused and smiled at the man. A vein started to throb in Terry's forehead.

With grace and a well-practiced understanding of how tenuous his position was, the concierge cut to the chase. "We have a self-guided tour to..." He looked around conspiratorially before continuing, "the fourth moon, where Kurtherian ruins pepper the landscape. The air is thin, but strapping youngsters like yourselves won't have any problems. You can sign up at registration."

Terry's lip twitched, but relaxed when the concierge excused himself after spotting another couple and making a beeline for them.

"We're on vacation," Char reminded TH.

"I don't suffer cheesedicks gladly."

Char leaned into him and wrapped an arm around his waist. He relaxed once again as they went to an open counter. "Live receptionists. I like it already," Terry whispered.

"But you wanted to throw the live concierge over a wall."

"I'm complicated," TH replied.

Char chose Shakespeare. "*As You Like It,* Act 5, Scene 1.

'The fool doth think he is wise, but the wise man knows himself to be a fool.'"

"I am *so* wise!" Terry declared. "Wait a minute. I'm such a fool! Wait. Sonofabitch."

"How can I make Venus more pleasurable for you?" the receptionist asked. Char bit her lip to keep from snorting.

"Check us in and hook us up with the Kurtherian getaway!" Terry smiled broadly at the young humanoid with a shimmering green tint to her skin. "Are you from Torregidor?"

"I am," the young female replied, beaming. She sparkled with her joy. "The tour. I have to share with you that no one goes on that tour."

"But that fucking guy brought it up." Terry stabbed a thumb over his shoulder while glowering mightily. His neck tensed with the effort of not turning his head to stare death daggers at the concierge. "He's quickly becoming my arch-nemesis."

"We're. On. Vacation," Char stated slowly and clearly. "Why doesn't anyone take that tour?"

"This is the Venus pleasure moon. Our guests want to be pampered and reside in absolute luxury for the time they are with us. To get to the ruins, you have to take a shuttle to Okkoto, a moon that is not comparable to Venus. It is inhospitable, to say the least."

"Sounds like the concierge was a genius when he offered it to us because that sounds exactly like something we'd like to do." Char thought for a moment. "How come there aren't scientists over there excavating, looking for Kurtherian secrets? Not even academics. A university or something?"

"Came and went decades ago," the clerk said. She handed a pair of light bracelets to Terry and Char. "Wear these, and you'll have access to all our facilities. You have reserved the honeymoon suite, so you're on the top level with an expansive view of everything we have to offer. Tomorrow, whenever you are ready, let us know, and we'll have the shuttle pick you up right off your balcony. A schedule of when the ruins on Okkoto are in daylight will be available on the screen in your room. Call if you need anything, and I mean *anything*. Venus is here for your pleasure."

"Do you have any single malt Scotch?" Terry asked, not risking Char's ire with an off-color joke toward the Torregidoran doing her job.

"Of course. All our suites have a fully stocked bar and an expansive selection from the food processor. An on-screen menu is provided."

"Food and drink. My husband will be in heaven."

The clerk pointed to a four-legged alien without a head. "He'll take your bag and lead you to your room."

Together they thanked the clerk. Terry was going to turn down the escort, but he was trying to relax and be pampered, as much as it went against his nature. He wanted to do it for Char. She wanted him to do it for himself.

They followed while the small alien trotted forward, two of his arms holding the bag in place on his back. They went through corridors that could have doubled as art galleries, which tickled their senses. Char pointed to a work that moved, sniffed, and touched a finger to the side of her nose. Terry could smell it, too. Their escort waited patiently.

Terry and Char walked around the piece slowly, appreciating the quality and how it engaged their minds.

The escort started up again when they finished, taking them past the elevators and around a corner, where a door blocked their way. Char waved her bracelet, and the door opened. Beyond was an elevator that required another wave to access it, and the three boarded, leaving little room to spare.

Next stop was the direct entrance to the honeymoon suite. Their escort let them go first into the room before dodging in, setting their bag on the floor, and disappearing before they could offer him a tip.

A panoramic view greeted them through the two-hundred-and-seventy-degree windows lining the walls of the round room. Two fireplaces burned, and overstuffed seating abounded. A large bedroom took up the last quarter of the room, and the bed was massive, with posts, curtains, and mirrors.

"No one can see in," Char read a notification by the windows.

"Nice penthouse, but still limited privacy, when the android is right here." Terry went to the bar. "One shot of each of your single malts. And do you have the All Guns Blazing beer called Your Dark Soul?"

"We have seventeen different single malts," the android warned. "And of course we have one of the most popular brews in the Etheric Federation. A stout with a hint of chocolate."

"The order stands. Line 'em up and let's see which ones are worth drinking."

"Our vacation, and you're doing shots?"

"*We're* doing shots. Tequila for the loveliest woman in all the galaxy, my robotic friend, and yes, I know androids aren't robots. If you're offended by that, you can go fuck yourself."

"You can call me whatever you wish. I was created to make Venus more pleasurable for you."

"For *us*," Terry corrected. Reluctantly, Char joined him at the bar.

"Wouldn't you be more comfortable looking out the window?" the android asked.

"We would," Char said, but Terry pointed to the bar. Char pointed to the window, so they compromised and sat by the window.

The android delivered their spirits and Terry made faces at the first six, waving them away after just a sip. On tasting the seventh, he hummed with delight, then went through the rest, just a sip each, and motioned for the android to take them all away. He saluted with the remaining shot glass. "Bring the bottle of..."

"Balvenie, sir. May I compliment your palette?"

"You may, and if I remember my history correctly, Balvenie was Gary Gygax's drink of choice. A double cask, oak and sherry for a smooth finish."

"Not that GaryCon thing again." Char smiled as she shook her head.

"Yes, that, but look at this view!"

The android took everything away, returning quickly with two bottles, one of Gran Patrón Platinum and the other, twelve-year-old Balvenie. The android disappeared into an alcove behind the bar to leave the couple in peace.

They clinked glasses and held hands as they observed the trees and gardens of the Cygnus VI pleasure moon, which disappeared into the distance on all sides. Small private shuttles moved people from the main building to outlying cabins, surrounded by dense hedges for maximum privacy.

There was no extreme to which Venus wouldn't go for their clients. Terry threw back his shot glass as Char matched him. "Bethany Anne would go to the ruins," Terry remarked.

"What is with your crush?" Char leaned back to get a better look at her husband.

"Not a crush," he shot back, holding his hands out defensively. "Just wondering, and I don't know why she's been on my mind. I think something must be happening somewhere."

Char closed her eyes and reached into the Etheric dimension. After a few moments, she blinked and looked at Terry. "I think you're right."

CHAPTER TWO

<u>***War Axe*, the Bad Company's Heavy Destroyer and Mobile Command Center**</u>

"Holy shit!" Christina shouted, jumping up and starting to dance. The RFP that had gotten Terry's attention got hers, too. "We're going to a major party!"

She sat down and read it again to make sure.

Flayse Conglomerate, Efluyez Homeworld, Alganor Sector

We request the presence of the Bad Company, in dress uniform, for a parade in the Flayse Magnate's honor. Flayse Conglomerate will pay half a million credits for this four-hour event. There will be no combat, although weapons will be carried as part of the parade.

Our sole purpose is to make the Homeworld's citizens proud of our abilities to conduct war, although we ourselves are always noncombatants. We wish our neighbor, the Frikanda Homeworld, to believe that we are not to be trifled with.

"Short and to the point," she said aloud. "Kai!"

"Yes, grandma?"

She did a backflip over the couch and shot like an

arrow across their quarters. Kai dove to the side, but too late; Christina grabbed a handful of his shirt and yanked him down. She twisted to get on top of him, and pinned his arms to his side, then bit his neck hard enough to draw blood.

"I'm not a grandma," she whispered into his ear before biting it.

"I give!" he called into the carpet before he started to chuckle. "That tickles."

She licked the drip of blood from his neck and climbed off. Christina didn't help him stand. She simply waited with her arms crossed.

Kai looked at her skeptically, and she flipped her hands out in the universal gesture for "Why?"

"Because I like the way you fight. You might be faster than me, and I find that titillating."

"'Might be?' If you aren't careful, you'll find yourself in here with a bistok as your roommate."

"A bistok. You know that video of you trying to wrestle that bistok is on the open net, right?"

"I have contracts out on the lives of those responsible," Christina deadpanned.

"You also know it was my mom."

"I know. If you ever break up with me, you will jeopardize the peace and well-being of your entire family."

Kai pulled at his collar and made a face. "I'm feeling a lot of pressure in our relationship, like one of us is needier than the other and it's sucking the air out of the room and making it hard to breathe and I feel like I'm swimming for the surface but can't quite get there and..."

Christina stopped him by holding a single finger in

front of his face. "Shall we break the good news to the others?"

"News of our impending marriage?"

"Hang on, Mister Clingy!" Christina shook her head. "The RFP. We need to make sure that everyone has a uniform. I know Terry Henry taught them how to march, but do they remember?"

"What's the delivery date?" Kai asked, turning serious.

"Oh, shit. Seven days."

Kai grimaced. "Transmit the acceptance, and I'll check our production facility to see if we have enough raw material to make dress uniforms. Would you know what that is? Do we have a pattern for a formal look?"

"Oh, shit," Christina repeated.

Kai gave her a stunned-carp look.

"Don't put this on me. Channel your inner grandpa and figure it out!" she declared triumphantly.

"Grandma," he whispered.

"So I'm a little bit older than you!" She pulled him close for a fierce kiss before spinning him around and slapping his backside. "You have work to do. Get on it. I'll be down in a bit. I need to research this place and make sure they aren't lying."

"Everyone lies, but about what?" Kai offered with a slight nod and made his way out.

Christina watched him go before turning back to the computer and digging up everything that General Smedley Butler, the *War Axe's* AI, knew about the Flayse Conglomerate.

. . .

Venus Pleasure Moon orbiting Cygnus VI

"Sun's up on Okkoto," Terry noted. Late morning greeted them with a flawless sunrise, followed by a substantial brunch served by their attendant android while they lounged before the windows, a crackling fireplace at their back. "I could get used to this."

"I'll take that as you getting used to vacations. I think we should take a week off every month."

"That's insane!" Terry tapped a pad with direct access to the Venus support team. "Please have our shuttle pick us up in thirty minutes."

The system acknowledged thirty minutes, followed by a one hour trip to Okkoto.

"What does a weekend look like on the *War Axe*?" Char asked pointedly.

"Two more work days until Monday." Terry's voice rose on the final word, making it sound like a question.

Char mumbled a reply before standing and dropping her robe as she strode boldly toward the magnificent bathroom with the shower that Terry had designated the "rain room" because of the way the water fell from the ceiling. Terry thought about it for a moment before tapping the pad.

"Make it an hour," he told the support team.

Terry wore his combat fatigues, a uniform he always had with him. What he didn't have were weapons other than his Ka-bar.

The Bad Company had the ability to produce any type

of edged weapon. Christina had designed a combination axe and pry bar to help when boarding an enemy ship. Some members carried kukris, a long and heavy curved knife. Terry had returned to the Ka-bar fighting knife of his Marine Corps days. He kept that with him at all times.

Char usually carried twin nine-millimeter pistols, but those, too, had been left on the *War Axe*. As a werewolf, she could always change into a fanged and deadly beast, so she never considered herself unarmed.

She wore a stylish khaki outfit with rugged hiking boots and a floppy safari hat.

Terry looked at the clothes as if he'd never seen them before. "Where'd you get those?"

"At a store. With *my* money." Her retort made Terry shake his head. "I refuse to dress like the only store I frequent is cash sales."

Cash sales. From the old U.S. military, where leftovers and turned-in uniforms could be purchased at a discount.

"I don't care about any of that, but it's almost like you knew we'd go hiking instead of spending the entire time in our swimsuits milling about private ponds."

Char shrugged noncommittally.

"Subterfuge!" Terry declared in a moment of inspiration. "You set this all up."

She pointed to the balcony where the shuttle was hovering, a short stair extended from an open hatch.

He winked. "And I love you that much more for it. If only I had my dog..."

"He's not your dog," Char clarified. "He's not anyone's dog. Well, maybe Cory's." Their daughter had lost her husband in the operation against the Skrima on Benitus

Seven. Dokken, the sentient German Shepherd, had done his best to fill the void and was now a constant companion.

"How about my wombat?"

"Floyd is all yours. She adores you."

Terry almost said it, but he refrained when Char gave him the side eye.

"After you," Terry said, motioning.

"Don't think that I don't know why you always ask me to go first up stairways."

"I know you know, but that doesn't change anything," Terry countered.

"I'm good with that," Char replied. She took three steps up and turned quickly to catch Terry staring at her ass. He blinked, smiled innocently, and followed her into the shuttle.

The flight attendant, another young female from Torregidor, offered them champagne, but they both deferred. Char asked for a glass of red wine, while Terry went with a bottle of Your Dark Soul. They sipped in silence as the shuttle left the atmosphere of the pleasure moon, skipped off the atmosphere of the planet around which the moons orbited, and assumed a measured approach to the fourth moon. Terry and Char pressed their faces against the windows to get the best view.

The shuttle flew slowly and silently over the ruins. Terry had expected an android to narrate like a tour guide, but they were given a blank slate upon which to draw their own conclusions. They had to see it for themselves.

Okkoto had probably been green once like Venus, but the Kurtherian ruins had come about because of a long-ago battle. The gleaming towers and city sprawl had been blasted by heavy weaponry, and little remained. Upstart weeds had taken root, but until the moon received a terraforming makeover, it would remain barely able to support life.

Before the shuttle landed, the attendant handed them each a heavy coat. Within, the pockets were filled with survival basics—water, food bars, high-strength rope, gloves, and more.

"Who were the Kurtherians at war with?" Terry asked, taking his coat and shrugging into it.

"Themselves," the attendant answered. "Here. Call when you're ready to be picked up. If you don't call, we'll be right here at dusk. You don't want to be on Okkoto when it's dark."

Terry took the device from her hand. "When is dusk?"

"The days are very long on Okkoto and the nights short. Dusk will be about forty hours from now."

Char put her jacket on when the shuttle landed, and the door opened. Cool air blasted through. She shivered and headed out with Terry right behind her.

They weren't on the moon more than a few heartbeats when the shuttle buttoned up and took off. Terry breathed deeply, having to work harder to pull less oxygen into his lungs. The lack of greenery kept the oxygen low.

"It wouldn't take much to get this place back up to speed where it would support life. There are a lot of settlers out there who would like to have a place of their own," Terry pondered.

The shuttle had dropped them in an open space that had once been near the center of the Kurtherian city. He slowly turned in a circle to take in what was left.

The silence of the breeze was unnerving. Without wildlife, nothing moved besides the weeds that fought the perpetual winds. No sounds reached them. When they talked, their voices were muffled.

"Not for the hearing impaired," Char noted.

"Which way shall we go, lover?" Terry asked happily. "I've heard that we're on vacation and it makes no difference how far or how fast we go as long as we enjoy the journey."

Char chuckled and pointed. "Now you're getting into the spirit, TH. You are the absolute worst person to buy a present for."

"Because I'm a *man*, baby!"

"I'll go with man-child," Char replied. She pointed in one direction for no better reason than it was the way she was facing.

"Anything screaming Etheric?" Terry asked while they walked at a leisurely pace. "The Kurtherians' stuff was long-lived. There has to be some residual energy."

Char stopped and relaxed, stretching out with her feelings to see if anything resonated, but there wasn't the slightest hint of anything pulling energy from the Etheric besides her and Terry Henry Walton.

"Zilch."

"I don't know if I'm supposed to feel relief at that or abject terror." Terry scratched his chin, as he did when he was deep in thought. "Shall we?"

He motioned toward the largest remains of a nearby structure.

"What do you think this was?" he asked.

"Whatever we want it to be." Char stopped and took in

the destroyed building along with those around it. "I see the city's council debating nonsensical issues as they postured to improve their own influence. I see harried clerks and bots managing the nuts and bolts of running the town. This used to be a beautiful place with caretakers lovingly nurturing the growth. Couples strolled hand in hand, enjoying life."

"I don't think the Kurtherians were like that at all. Besides the posturing bit, that is." Terry glanced left and right, expecting to see furtive movements, but there was nothing. They were the only living creatures on Okkoto.

"A Kurtherian civil war, where nothing is civil. It's just war."

"When politics fail," Terry scowled. "Enough of that! Where do you think they hid their cafeteria?"

"The ground floor? The basement? Higher?"

"That's no help at all." Terry tipped his head toward the once-broad set of stairs that led into the structure. "Definitely a government building."

"Maybe an art gallery?" Char stopped when she reached the last stair without rubble and looked for a way inside.

"I've never heard of an archaeological dig here, or that this place even existed. Is it such routine news that there are Kurtherian ruins?"

"That is a good question," Char conceded. "I didn't know about this place until I started digging. It seems to be nothing more than a footnote to the Venus love shack."

Terry chuckled. He walked back and forth in front of what used to be the building's entrance. On the far right side, the fallen stone-like masonry had a gap that wasn't as high or as loose as the rest of it.

He clambered up and stood at the top of the depression. "No matter where it started, the cafeteria is now in the basement. Just like the penthouse."

Char scrambled up the loose stone. Terry wasn't kidding.

"Looks like a missile hit it from this side and blew out a huge section of the supporting structure. The rest of it collapsed."

"How many floors?"

Terry shrugged before holding up two fingers, followed by five. "I know nothing about Kurtherian architecture, but we're about to find out. It doesn't look like any formal excavations took place here. Let's see what there is to see."

Char removed her rope from her jacket and tied it around the remains of a stanchion. They used it to back down a loose pile and into the rubble below. At the bottom, they found the ground to be stable. Various remnants of broken furniture stuck out from nooks and crevices, but they didn't find any technology.

"You'd think there would be something."

Char pulled Terry to her. "There doesn't have to be anything. The thought of what was here is enough. We are on a journey of discovery, are we not? One foot on sea and one on shore, to one thing constant never."

"*Much Ado About Nothing*, but here there is something to do."

Terry ducked to look beneath a massive slab. He found a flashlight in his jacket that held all things, as if the resort had known, and shined it into a small hole.

"There's empty space." He pointed into the opening.

"As in, anything that fell in there may have survived the wreckage and the violence of time," Char said.

Terry stood and flexed his biceps in the Mister Universe pose. "Think we can move this, lover mine?"

Char stretched her shoulders and her back, then squatted next to Terry and got a grip. "Remember, lift with your legs." She winked.

"On two. One. Two." Together they surged, and the slab moved with their effort. After they lifted it above their knees, Terry grunted. "I don't think I can hold it for you to take a look."

"And we can't push it forward because we'll fall in the hole," Char managed through the labor of holding the slab.

"Move sideways, your direction. We'll slide it off."

Char immediately started shuffling her feet, keeping the lateral strain from her knees. Terry pushed her way.

"Letting go on one," Char gritted out. Terry nodded, but she didn't see. "One."

She pushed the slab away from her and jumped back, but Terry was a millisecond too late, and he started to go down. He let go and fell face-first onto the slab before rolling into the hole.

CHAPTER THREE

The *War Axe*, Keeg Station, Dren Cluster

"What do you think of this?" Kai asked. Christina sighed.

"You know Terry Henry. If we fuck this up, he'll have our asses. We'll be scrubbing the hull of the *War Axe* using nothing but our toothbrushes," Christina muttered.

"What's the big deal? If he doesn't like them, we can change."

"The big deal is that there will be video and images across the galaxy of the Bad Company on parade. We've never done that before. If we embarrass him, we'll never hear the last of it."

"How about this?" Kai brought up an image from the old Earth archive. "It says Marine Corps Officers' Mess Dress. Isn't that what we want?" The image showed a coat that was dark blue to the point of being black. A red cummerbund sat atop a white shirt. The coat was buttoned at the top and spread open toward the trousers, which had a scarlet and gold stripe from belt to shoe along the outside.

"That looks like it was made for old men with growing mid-sections, but look here. This is a dress uniform, too." Christina pointed at an image of a jacket with gold buttons that was dark with red piping. Dark blue trousers with the same stripe completed the outfit.

"How in the holy hell is that going to look on an Ixtali? Or better yet, a Podder?"

"A Yollin?" Christina snickered at the thoughts. "That's the one we're going with. Get everyone in here to get fitted."

"*You* get them here, Colonel," Kai shot back. "I'm a simple civilian, little more than an indentured servant."

"Sucks being the boss' grandson? Is that what you're saying?"

"There *are* perks," he said softly as he made eyes at the Were.

"If you weren't so damn good-looking, I might put you in your place. Until then, my husky hunk of man candy, you prepare the process, and I'll bring the grist to your mill."

With a quick peck on the cheek, Christina stood up and walked away. Her eyes unfocused as she used the comm chip implanted in her head to send the message to all hands. *All members of the Bad Company are recalled. We have a mission that requires two weeks of training, and we have six days to make that happen. Those warriors currently on the* War Axe, *report to the hangar deck immediately...*

. . .

Okkoto, the Fourth Moon Orbiting Cygnus VI

Terry curled into a ball as he fell and groaned when he hit after less than a heartbeat of falling. He looked up; it was only five meters to the opening. Char's head appeared.

"I'm fine," Terry said too quickly, wincing as he stood. A rib was out of place, and he twisted until it snapped back to where it was supposed to be. His stomach muscles spasmed with the pain before the nanocytes provided the relief of rapid healing. "No, really."

"Throw me your rope," she told him, ignoring his defensiveness about how badly he'd been hurt.

He tossed it up and then shined his flashlight, which had survived the short fall and impact without any issue. Landing on it had left a dent in Terry's body, but not the flashlight.

He was standing on a metal barrier that could have been the top of an elevator car. A rope slapped down before Char landed next to him, her knees flexed to absorb the impact of the jump.

Terry looked at the rope.

"For climbing out." She knelt to look closer at the metal. "Elevator?"

"My thoughts exactly. Is this an escape hatch?" A hair-thin outline was visible once Terry had brushed away the dust with the toe of his boot.

Char leaned close, and with her fingers, whisked the area clean. She cleared an obstruction from the side and pulled out a release lever. "Shall we?" she asked, using Terry's phrase.

"Please do," Terry replied.

Char twisted the handle and it popped, releasing a

cloud of gas. Char jumped to her feet. Terry caught her and shoved her against the wall, putting his body between her and the trap door.

Nothing else happened.

Terry took a breath. "Smells like stale air."

He moved to the opening, which was large enough for him to pass through, and shined his light down.

"Not sure what I'm looking at."

Char laid down next to him and peered inside.

The contraption jerked and started to drop, and they held each other to keep from falling through the hole. They accelerated as they descended. A door slammed shut over their heads, leaving them in darkness lit only by the small beam of the flashlight. Dust flitted through the air.

Their bodies lifted off the top of the elevator as it dropped faster and faster. Terry and Char both tensed. "This is gonna hurt," Terry managed through clenched teeth. He worked his arm under his face and Char mirrored his pose as they prepared to hit bottom.

The *War Axe*, Keeg Station, Dren Cluster

"I can't move my head," Gefelton complained.

"These uniforms suck," somebody grumbled.

"Embrace the suck!" Kimber repeated a saying her father used at the most inappropriate times. She did a double-take. "What are *you* bitching about?"

Gefelton pointed to the clasp that held the stiff high-neck collar in place, which was digging into his neck.

"If we change that to something weaker, it'll pop, and your collar won't stay in place. It's like that so you hold your head high and keep your eyes straight ahead," Kimber explained.

"What if we get into a fight?" he pressed.

"No one is fighting in these uniforms."

"You got *that* right," the second voice muttered.

Kimber jumped onto the short counter that they'd set up to help issue the uniforms. "Crybabies, whiners, complainers, and purple-headed toads…" She glared at the group, who looked uncomfortable yet indifferent. "I don't know where I was going with that."

She stopped to collect her thoughts. Someone laughed before grunting in pain.

"Oh, yeah." She remembered. "If you aren't complaining, you aren't training. If warriors aren't complaining, they aren't happy! So you pack of sandy buttholes must be the happiest and most effective fighting force in the whole universe."

Kimber used all of her self-discipline to resist pulling at her collar, which was starting to chafe, and looked down at Kai behind the counter. She couldn't take it anymore.

"Kai," she said softly. "Oversize the collars so each warrior can stick four fingers between the collar and their neck. Any tighter than that and the blood will be cut off to their brains. That probably wouldn't affect most of them, but they need to stay in step while we march in parade."

She turned back to the warriors, shocked at her sudden concession. "Hey, you goofy bastards! We only have to tolerate these things for four hours, which means you need to be ready to wear them for eight. Turn in your jackets, square your shit away, and get back here. We start practice drill on the hangar deck in one hour."

Kimber jumped down as Christina appeared in the doorway.

"We're getting them resized a hair." Kimber held her fingers close together to show how minimal the alterations would be. "What are we going to do with our four-legged warriors?"

"When Terry Henry gets back, we'll figure out if we can do a dress uniform that will look appropriate on all our people. But for this one, they're going to have to sit it out."

"They probably aren't going to like that," Kimber replied.

"They are going to be the envy of everyone." Christina nodded toward the crowd, who was happily holding their jackets in their hands, necks red or worse, rubbed raw. "I'm envious."

Kimber snickered as she yanked her collar open and started to rip her jacket off. "I expect you're right. Are you coming to drill with us?"

Okkoto, the Fourth Moon Orbiting Cygnus VI

The elevator rose to meet them, now falling slower than Terry and Char. They pressed against the unknown metal as it decelerated significantly and finally stopped. A door within the elevator popped open.

"Go through, or try to find a way back up?" Terry shined the light back up the shaft, which seemed to rise forever. They couldn't tell where the door had cut them off from the surface. Everything was lost in the haze.

Terry checked the comm device to call for the shuttle.

"No joy," he said when there was no signal. "The air looks clear in there."

Char followed his flashlight beam. "I don't think the way out is up there." She pointed and shook her head. "And before you ask, I did not set this up. We were just supposed to walk around and check out ruins. Simple, but that's what you do on vacation—not take death-defying falls a thousand feet down an elevator shaft."

"You think we fell a thousand feet?"

Char rolled her eyes.

"I get you," Terry conceded. "But it could have easily been five hundred. We fell a long way."

"I'll go first," Char said and was halfway through the hatch before Terry could protest. She dropped lightly to the floor and waited for her husband to follow. He landed next to her and took a step forward to block the doors with his body before shining the light down a short passage that turned sharply.

Char walked through and stopped. Terry watched her closely.

"A *lot* of energy being pulled from the Etheric down here. It's bad," she told him.

"Like Benitus-Seven-vortex-to-Hell-bad or just some-heavy-machinery-with-a-few-Kurtherians bad?"

She shook her head.

"If those ginormous throbbing ass-munchers are down here, TH, you'd better be ready to beat them six ways till Sunday with a bent pencil," a familiar voice said from the corridor before them. Their heads snapped to the sound.

In a glossy black suit of form-fitting armor stood Bethany Anne, Queen of High Tortuga, one of the most powerful people known, and a vampire who could channel Etheric energy almost like magic. She watched them, mildly amused by their looks of confusion.

Terry started to bow, but Char stopped him.

"How did you get down here?" Char asked.

"That is a damn good question. One minute, I'm with my kids, and the next I'm standing here listening to you two plan your next honeymoon." Bethany Anne tapped the side of her head. "TOM? ADAM?" She exhaled as she looked around. "Great. You two fuckers picked a wonderful time to take a vacation."

"We weren't planning anything," Terry replied feebly before shaking his head and straightening up. "We need to get out of here. I think the shaft was a trap, but it's too late for recriminations on my miscue of jumping in to check things out. We're on Okkoto, the fourth moon circling Cygnus VI. There are the ruins of a Kurtherian city up top, but it was destroyed a long time ago in a civil war of some sort. That's it—all we know, my Queen."

"Cut the Queen shit, TH," BA snapped. "It's BA to my friends, and you've known that for over a century. The questions are, what is pulling so much Etheric energy down here, and what are you two going to do about it?"

"I thought the question was, how do we get out of here?" Terry offered before adding, "BA."

Char laughed softly. "There's only one way to go. Let us take the lead." Char stepped away, nodding as she passed the Queen. Terry followed, smiling as he went.

"I guess if we have to be trapped five hundred feet below the surface of a moon in some Kurtherian outpost, we couldn't have asked for better company."

"I could say the same thing," BA replied tactfully, "although I think John would come in handy. He would love this shit."

"He punched me in the face," Terry said gently.

"He's punched a lot of people in the face," she replied as she shrugged. "Don't take it personally."

"I didn't," Terry answered. He and Char peeked around the corner and saw a long corridor with regularly-spaced doors and frequent passages branching off. "This is going to take a while. Want to split up?"

He turned, but BA hadn't followed. He rushed back to the corner, but she wasn't there either.

"Where..." Terry started to ask. "What the fuck is going on?"

"My dislike for this place is growing with each heartbeat." Char scowled.

"Did we just see Bethany Anne?" Terry asked, still confused.

"*I* saw her." Char was convinced.

"As did I." Terry shined his flashlight back and forth for one last look. "What was she wearing?"

"Looked like some new battle armor. It was badass and emphasized her shape. I want some like that."

"I'll put Smedley on it the second we get back. We *will* get back to the *War Axe*."

"If you say it, you have to make it happen."

Terry walked briskly to the first door and tried it, but it wouldn't open. There was only a panel to the side, no handle. It was, after all, Kurtherian-made, and they didn't waste time turning doorknobs.

"You said the power is on down here?" Terry asked, still

relying on his flashlight. "Lights on!"

Nothing happened.

"Maybe you have to say it in Kurtherian," Char suggested.

"I don't speak Kurtherian."

"Then it appears that we're shit out of luck. How long do you think the batteries will last?"

"I hope it's about forty hours."

"Why forty?"

"That's when the shuttle from Venus arrives to pick us up. I hope they look for us. Our ropes should lead them to the shaft. They can blast it open and get to us."

Char wasn't so sure they would look that hard since the ruins sprawled. Or that they would be that diligent in trying to get them out. She wondered how long it would take before Christina and the *War Axe* came looking for them.

No amount of pushing or pulling changed the fact that none of the doors would open.

"I guess we have to find a different way than brute force," Terry offered.

"Channel your inner Ted," Char replied.

"I love that guy. And then there's the rest of the time when he chaps my ass."

"He didn't choose to be that way. Once you get past the all-business veneer, he is as much one of us as anyone else."

"I know," Terry replied. "He's done more for all of us than anyone else, but he's not here, so it's up to us."

"Don't get hurt, because Cory's not here either."

"Nobody's here."

"Just BA and me. I'll tell her you called both of us 'nobody.'"

"Hang on, hot mama, you know what I meant." Terry eyed her suspiciously.

"Words, TH. Use them wisely."

Char didn't seem at all perturbed by the situation. Terry started to suspect that it was all a setup—the purple-eyed werewolf and the Queen conspiring to get his goat.

Terry relaxed. "Try this corridor?" He pointed to the left. "We'll keep taking lefts until eventually we've circum-navigated the entire place. I expect we'll find a way out."

Char patted her pockets. "Four nutrition bars and two liters of water."

"Same here," Terry confirmed. "Forty hours' worth and then some, if we stretch it. What did Kurtherians eat?"

"Food?" Char shrugged. "Unless we figure out how to get these doors open, we won't know anything."

"Let's follow the corridors before we start breaking things." Terry was starting to think of the underground as an amusement park, there for wealthy clients to live an adventure, like that old show *Westworld* on television.

Terry took off at a good clip, waving a hand in front of doors as he passed. He tried them all but didn't expect any to open. The corridor ended with a T intersection, so Terry turned left. They passed six more doors, three on each side, mirroring each other, but none opened as he passed. The corridor ended at a double door.

"I think we can get these open," he said over his shoulder. He jammed his fingertips against the center crease where the doors butted tightly against each other, then stood close and pulled. Terry groaned with the effort until a small gap appeared, wedged his fingers in to give himself more leverage pulling outward, and doubled his efforts. The doors popped and rocketed into the frame on each side.

Terry's arms went straight out to the sides, and he stumbled forward into a large room filled with various equipment. Red eyes blinked to life, and a pencil-thin laser lanced through the air and burned a hole into and through the human's chest. Terry yowled in surprise and jumped to the side, leaving a trail of smoke from his clothes and the stench of burnt flesh.

Char ran into the room and dove to the right. She hit and rolled, then scrambled behind a metal stanchion.

Terry was doing the same thing on the left side of the room, but his wheezing was giving him away. The hole the laser had burned through his lung had not yet sealed. Char picked an empty flask from a table behind her, stood up, and threw it.

The plastiglass flew straight and true and smashed into the bot's head, and it turned and fired its laser pistol. She was already down and looking for different cover when a metal table screeched as it was pushed across the floor and rammed into the bot.

Terry stood, lifting the table and slamming the heavy top like a pile driver into the bot's chest frame. It arced and sparked electric blue through the metal table. Terry flew backward, bounced off a stand, and rolled to the floor. Char ran for the bot, picked up the laser weapon, and drilled a series of holes into the thing. When she was sure it was dead, she rushed to her husband, only to find him unconscious.

She rolled him over, produced one of her water bags, and poured a few drops into his mouth. He relaxed as the nanos went to work healing him.

"Way to kick that hunk of fucking metal's ass!" Bethany Anne clapped until she saw Terry Henry on the floor. "TH, what the sweet hell are you doing down there?"

Char listened to his chest. "Yes." She sighed in relief, rubbing her face against TH's perpetual stubble. "He's going to be okay."

"Give it a few, and he'll be back in the land of the living. I'd say he had a little too much AC/DC, but then we'd have *Thunderstruck* in our heads for the rest of the day."

Char continued to cradle her husband's head.

"What has it been, TH, a hundred and fifty-six years since you received your nanocytes?" BA asked as if Terry Henry weren't unconscious. "But you two have created something special. I think Ted is trying to patent your modified nanos."

"Ted is doing *what*?"

"I'm only pulling your leg, or at least I think I am. Who knows with Ted?" BA waved one hand indiscriminately.

Terry moaned as he opened his eyes, but the corners of his mouth twitched up in the best smile he could manage.

"How much did you pay for this amusement park ride, because I want our money back. That fucker drilled a hole through my chest."

"What?" Char was confused.

"Didn't you set this up?"

"No. If I could have, I would have, but there is no secret exit and no safe word. We are trapped who knows how far underground in an abandoned Kurtherian complex. We are knee deep in the shit, TH, which for us is business as usual. I have high hopes that we'll find a way out, but if it gets any more dangerous, we may get killed before we see daylight again."

Terry struggled to stand, even with Char's help. "BA," he grumbled, "we could have used your help."

"Sorry, TH. Got here about five seconds too late."

"Where were you?"

"I wish I could answer that. I was on High Tortuga, then all of a sudden I was here, a shitload of light years away. Then I wasn't here, and then I was again. Fuck if I know. When you two cracked the seal on this place, it sent shock waves through the Etheric. Way to go, fuckstick." Bethany Anne turned to Char to spread her annoyance. "You too, Mrs. Fuckstick."

"How in the hell was I supposed to know?" TH argued. "This place was dead. D.E.A.D, Dead."

"I'll let it slide this one time," Bethany Anne quipped. "But don't do it again."

"I promise. Until then, I'm going to take great pleasure in taking their greatest secrets while also fucking shit up, like that ass-monkey." Terry nodded toward the dead robot.

"Who took down the bot while you were taking a nap?" BA chided.

Char waved the handheld laser. "We have a weapon."

"At least one." Terry smiled at his wife. "Any ideas what this place is?" Terry asked.

BA's head tracked around the room. "Looks like a lab," she offered. "Science shit." BA nodded in the direction of the bot. "Anything running besides your buddy?"

"My buddy met an untimely end, but its very existence suggests that there are other things down here with power. We probably have to find those while also avoiding them." Terry looked at the floor as his breathing slowed with his healing lung. "We need to turn the lights on so we can find the stairway out of here. There has to be an emergency exit. If not, we need the elevator we rode down to go back up."

"Who says it hasn't already?" BA asked.

Terry's face dropped and he hurried for the door, and Char ran after him. Shining their one flashlight before them and running like their hair was on fire, they covered the ground quickly.

CHAPTER FOUR

The *War Axe*, Keeg Station, Dren Cluster

The Pods that the Bad Company's Direct Action Branch called their dropships reloaded into the launch tubes. The shuttles usually used to transport warriors on liberty were still involved with the reconstruction of Keeg Station.

The menagerie of humans and aliens marched out the back of the Pods, down the ramp, and into the hangar bay. Most had backpacks or small duffels. A couple looked like someone had picked them up out of a bar's cleaning sump and dragged them face-down to the station's transit bay.

Which may have been the case.

"Cap?" Kimber inquired. "Got everyone?"

"Eighteen for eighteen, Major," Sergeant Capples replied.

"Dump their trash in their rooms and get them back down here to be fitted for their parade uniforms."

"I'm not sure most of them are fit for anything right now, but I'll have 'em back in ten," the sergeant joked.

"Eight," Kimber countered.

"Eight it is." Capples ran to the hatch to get in front of the mob before they disappeared from sight. "Listen up, you gutterslugs! The major has given you eight minutes to dump your shit and get back here. Clock starts now!"

The three who carried nothing leaned against the bulkhead, then sat, and finally curled up and went to sleep.

Capples followed the others into the ship, and footsteps pounding up the stairs echoed from the open hatch.

Christina joined Kimber in the hangar bay where the rest of the Bad Company were taking a break. They had already started drill practice, and none of them were happy.

"There's no rush," Christina said.

"I know." Kimber smiled devilishly. "But nothing cures a hangover like an adrenaline rush."

"Tried and true. By the way, I thought the station was all construction all the time and there was no partying going on."

Kimber rolled her head sideways to look at the colonel. "I've been with the Force de Guerre and then the Bad Company for almost as long as both have existed. I've never seen a warrior who couldn't find a party."

Christina accepted the naked truth.

"This gig." Kimber changed gears. "Five hundred grand just for showing up? There's going to be one hell of a bash when we get back to the ship."

"Given they're offering that many credits, there's something they aren't telling us. I think we should fly our fighters over the formation, and half the formation should be armored."

"The RFP was clear—just us in dress uniforms."

"What if their show of force is wiping out the Bad Company's Direct Action Branch?"

Abandoned Kurtherian Outpost, Okkoto, the Fourth Moon Orbiting Cygnus VI

Terry and Char arrived at the elevator shaft to find the door closed. Terry jammed his fingers into the seam and pulled, but it refused to give.

"Should have blocked it with something," Terry noted.

"Makes it more imperative that we restore power."

Terry pursed his lips. "Dammit! Where'd BA go?"

"I'm not sure she's really here. I think she's in and out of the Etheric dimension."

"But the Etheric is real. It provides power for a lot of our stuff, so if she's in the Etheric, she's still real and I'm not making up our short conversations." Terry waited a moment before adding, "Am I?"

Char snorted. "I hear her too. She called us knuckleheads, so I think it's her."

"Maybe it's an exotic defensive program designed by the Kurtherians to give us something we respect. What if she asks us to jump off a ledge as a leap of faith? I'd love to follow her orders, but she'll need to understand that we may be skeptical."

"Then you won't be following her orders," Char countered.

"Fuck me." Terry ran his hand through his hair and scowled at the floor. "You're not yanking my chain?"

"No. I set up the tour and even the obnoxious concierge

to plant the seed, but nothing else. No one knew this place was here."

"It looks more twenty-first-century human sci-fi than Kurtherian. I would have thought it would be more..." He searched for the right word. "Advanced?"

"More science fiction than science fiction?" Char offered. She started to head back down the corridor. "We better find some water, too. I don't think we'll be leaving anytime soon."

Terry's scowl changed to a look of grim determination. With conspiracy theories and imaginary Queens in his rearview mirror, he could focus on the task at hand. "We need to get out of here, and the exit is up that shaft." He nodded over his shoulder while shining his flashlight past Char.

She didn't see the nod but was of the same mind.

"Goddammit, TH!" Char blurted. "We're supposed to be on fucking vacation. I'm supposed to be getting a massage and a coffee scrub while you go snorkeling or something."

"I'm sorry," he muttered, unsure of what changed in the last four seconds.

"No, you're not. To get you to relax, we can't do normal relaxing stuff, like shop for shoes or sit on a beach and sip Mai Tais."

"We did the Mai Tai thing for a long damn time," he argued. "Fifty years. I've had my last Mai-fucking-Tai!"

He hurried to get in front of his wife and turned to face her, blocking the passage with his body.

"This isn't helping us escape." She glared at him.

"We're different, but better together, Char," he said

softly. "I like this shit—as long as it doesn't kill us. I can't stand shopping for shoes, but you and Cory are more than welcome to do as much of that as you can handle. Don't take that as a challenge, by the way.

"I'm not sure what the balance is. We work a lot because the Federation is huge and there are too few of us who can be trusted with keeping the peace. Maybe we should turn it all over to Christina and retire, but without the Bad Company, I don't know what I'd do with myself. Maybe become the next All Guns Blazing brewmaster and beer magnate?"

Char shook her head. "If there are any Kurtherians down here, they are going to be appalled that they are losing the war against fucked-up people like us."

"And that is the sweetest victory of all," Terry declared.

"I forgive you for being you."

"I'm not sure that's what I was going for."

"I'm just mad because we're stuck down here and my plans for a great vacation are shot to hell."

"That is something we can agree on." Terry turned around and walked side by side with Char as they returned to the one door they could open. It was now closed, too. "For fuck's sake! Get your laser pistol ready."

Terry's face turned red as he pried the door apart. This time, he was ready for when it released and didn't fall through. When the interior lights came on, he dodged out of the way.

The *War Axe*, Keeg Station, Dren Cluster

"How can we make this suck more?" someone up front asked. Kimber stood stock-straight. The extra space in her collar relieved the chafing, but it did nothing to ease the general discomfort.

"The good ol' days of the Corps," she mumbled so that only Christina could hear.

"Shared misery to build the team. Is that the only lesson TH took away from his time in the Marines? We share an absolute butt-ton of misery around this place."

"We have great parties!" Kimber declared.

"Can't argue about that. If it was easy, everyone would be doing it. Seems like our people are very popular at the seediest dives," Christina remarked.

"I think that is a constant through the ages. The harder the rite of passage to get in, the more they eschew the finer things in life."

"What do you think your parents are doing right now?"

Kimber winced. "Jumping snack packs! They're on their nine hundredth honeymoon. What do you *think* they're doing?"

"I didn't mean that. You know your dad. There's no way he's hanging out by a pool while your mom gets a massage."

"He did it for a long, long time way back when, and he swore he'd never do it again. I believe him. Mom? She's wily. I'm sure she had something planned."

Christina shook her head as the warriors tumbled through the hatch by the stairs on their way back into the hangar. "Cap was right. This bunch isn't fit for anything." She stormed toward them. "Hey, motherfuckers!"

• • •

Abandoned Kurtherian Outpost, Okkoto, the Fourth Moon Orbiting Cygnus VI

Char dove to the left of the open doors, snatching glances inside. No one shot at her and no new bots appeared.

But the lights were on.

"Somebody knows we're here," Terry said softly, stealing his own furtive looks into the laboratory. He finally stood and walked through the door, but with knees flexed and his paces short so he could react more quickly. His eyes darted everywhere and back again. "What's different besides the lights?"

Char followed him in, laser pistol in her hand. She went right and Terry left and they scoured the room, looking for a terminal or place from where they would interact with the system.

Maybe even find a map.

"Mr. Kurtherian Outpost, could you please tell us how to get back to the surface?" Terry asked, an eyebrow raised and his head cocked as he waited for an answer.

Continued silence was what he had been expecting. The outpost would give him no help. Terry leaned close to the destroyed robot. "There are things like beakers, but no tools. Nothing to stir chemicals, no measuring containers, no burners, and definitely no hardware like hammers or screwdrivers. It's like they prepared the lab, but the scientists never moved in."

He checked the pockets of his jacket for a multi-tool and was surprised to find one. He knew he shouldn't have been. The jacket was designed for survival, and a standard multi-tool was a must-have.

Terry used his tool to dismantle the bot, finding a critical section that had been crushed in his attack using the metal table. He wanted to take something from the complex to give to Ted and the other researchers at R2D2 to see if there was anything they could reverse-engineer. He waved Char to him. There were no wires inside the creation. Together, they still had no idea.

"This part?" Char asked doubtfully.

Terry told Char, "As good as any, but I don't know how that's helping us get out of here. In my mind, getting out is a foregone conclusion. I don't want to go empty-handed since I suspect when we find the way out, we'll take it and not be able to come back for anything."

"I hope that's true. Grab it and let's go. Maybe the place will start lighting up on its own. I'd like to see what's behind some of these doors."

"Me, too, lover," Terry agreed after ripping the technological heart out of the robot. With other equipment in the room but nothing that could be easily carried, they left the rest of it behind. "Staying to the left, just like when I used to play Castle Wolfenstein."

Char was in front of him, and he didn't need to see to know how hard she rolled her eyes.

He trolled along the left wall, but there weren't features or alcoves, just a smooth wall of a material Terry couldn't identify. They passed the T intersection and continued down a hall with three more sets of doors opposite each other but no end door. Terry and Char tried each one, but nothing moved. When they reached the dead end, they backtracked, trying the doors that the other had tried.

When they reached the T, they turned down it. "That's

one down and who knows how many left." The light of their one flashlight remained stalwart through the darkness. "No dust."

"I don't hear anything, but the air handling systems have to be working. The air is clean."

Terry sniffed first before closing his eyes and listening carefully.

"I don't hear a thing. Everything has to be automated. There can't be anything alive down here. There's no dander. No waste, no dust. Maybe this place was sealed so well that the air is clean, but not because of air handling..." Terry's thought drifted where he didn't want to go—another threat to their lives.

"Then we have a limited air supply, depending on how big this place is." Char put their predicament into words.

"How long will our nanocytes keep us alive without air to breathe?"

"How long did you have when you lost your suit containment back on that station, you and Dokken?" Char asked.

"Minutes." Terry pursed his lips and took slow, deep breaths. "I guess we better pick up the pace, then. I miss Dokken."

Dokken was a sentient German Shepherd thanks to the Pod-doc injecting him with nanocytes and implanting a communications chip in his brain. He was a son of Ashur, Bethany Anne's dog.

Char nodded and Terry stepped off first, taking a left at the intersection that had they turned right, would have taken them back to the elevator shaft.

Doors were spaced regularly on both sides of the corridor, and Terry waved his hand at the first one on the left. When it opened, he jumped back, and Char brought her pistol up.

CHAPTER FIVE

The lights came on as the door slid to the side. Terry risked a glance, but only saw heavy cabinetry within. Char looked through the doorway from the other side, craning her neck to see from different angles.

The door started to slide shut, and Terry's hand shot out to grab it. It dutifully retracted back into the wall and Terry eased himself around the corner, the door pocket at his back. The room was austere except for the cabinets, which upon closer inspection appeared to be casings.

"These look like those power supply boxes that we found on the abandoned Benitus station," Terry said.

"Where we learned how long Dokken could go without air."

"But we saved him!" Terry declared while studying what was in the room. No control panels, no decorations, no way to access information from the boxes.

"Dokken was taped to your face to create a seal."

"That bastard licked my mouth," Terry replied. "I won't do it again."

"You know you would."

Terry reached for the box, wondering if touching it might bring up a holographic interface. An angry red aura appeared around his hand, yanking and pulling before throwing him into the wall. He bounced and staggered but stayed upright.

"Shielded," Char said unnecessarily. "Usually, the shield just blocks you. What was going on with that first part before you got tossed?"

Terry blinked and grunted as he worked his muscles to make sure nothing was discombobulated. "Seemed like it was trying to pull me in, but it hurt like my hand was in lava."

"I'd say let it pull you in, but if it's going to punish you during the process, that probably isn't an option."

"Getting trapped inside a force field surrounding a nondescript box? No, that wouldn't be my first choice."

"We might need to try it at some point," Char suggested, wincing at the desperation that would lead them to such a drastic action.

"But not yet," Terry confirmed. When they stepped back into the hall, the lights blinked into existence, bathing the corridors in soft light. "It's what we wanted, but now I'm not sure I want it."

The skin crawled on Char's neck. She kept a firm grip on the laser pistol as her senses discovered something that hadn't been there before. "What's that sound?"

The *War Axe*, Keeg Station, Dren Cluster

"Preparing to Gate. All hands, we are leaving Keeg

Station. Say goodbye, and if everything goes according to plan, we'll be back in less than a week," Captain Micky San Marino announced over the ship-wide broadcast.

"Why'd he have to jinx it?" Christina asked. Kimber looked down and shook her head.

When the major looked up, the warriors were shuffling and wiggling. Her patience instantly evaporated, and she stormed into their ranks. "You are practicing standing still, which clearly means you need more practice!" she bellowed. "Lock your nasty bodies up, and I better not see anyone move. Exercise some self-discipline, people!"

She trolled the ranks, back and forth, daring someone to move. The warriors remained statue still.

Kimber returned to where Christina was standing in front of the formation. They all wore their dress uniforms. Some of those who had been on liberty were starting to sweat. Too much alcohol, not enough water, and no sleep. Their bodies were starting to rebel.

"You might want to think about lightening up," Christina suggested. "You seem a bit high-strung."

Kimber turned to the taller woman. "Maybe, but we have six days left to pull this off. I have no idea if we'll make it. Dad will be pissed if we dick up a parade in uniforms that he used to wear."

"Fair enough. How long are you going to keep them like that?"

"This go? An hour. A fifteen-minute break, and then two hours. If they don't screw that up too badly, we'll call it a day and start tomorrow at five in the morning."

"That sounds like the cost of screwing it up, not the reward for success."

"Six?"

"That's more like it." Christina kept her hands behind her. She was as miserable as those in formation, but she could move around when she had to. "Poor sops. But a cool half a mil. Bonuses for everyone."

"What the hell do you think you're doing?" Kimber demanded of one of the warriors and hurried away.

Abandoned Kurtherian Outpost, Okkoto, the Fourth Moon Orbiting Cygnus VI

"Something's coming," Terry said, looking desperately for cover. He motioned back the way they'd come. Char turned and ran about thirty meters, and Terry sprinted past her as they turned the corner of the first T intersection. She stopped and threw her back against the wall, then crouched to aim down the corridor with her laser pistol.

Terry leaned over her and peeked down the now well-lit corridor. He turned off his flashlight and tucked it into a coat pocket without taking his eyes away from the direction the sound was coming from.

Their superlative hearing, thanks to the nanos, gave them warning when a normal person would have been caught unaware. A nearly silent flying bot appeared, but it used a physical propulsion system. Char could feel that it was powered by the Etheric, but Terry didn't know or care. He suspected its purpose was offensive in nature, as in, it was a security device. His hand still stung from the angry red forcefield.

The device skipped past the room they'd gone into and headed straight for them.

"Fire!" Terry shouted as it approached. Char had the same thought, and she drilled the device as the call to action left his lips.

The laser was stymied by an energy shield, so the beam stopped cold well before it reached the floating bot. The security device counter-fired, hitting the pistol in Char's hand and exploding the device. Char was thrown back, and she clutched her face as she rolled.

Terry had been leaning over Char and took the majority of the blast in his exposed abdomen. He popped straight up, coming off his feet to land on his face. He grunted as he hit and immediately rolled away as a second beam scorched the spot where his head had just been. Terry launched himself at the opposite wall, hitting it with his feet and pushing off as he threw himself at the bot. He drove his knife down toward it. It caught in the forcefield, but like he was pushing it through soft wood, he was able to keep the blade moving.

But so slowly. The muscles in his arm bulged with the effort, and his abs screamed for relief. Terry grabbed the hilt with his other hand and screamed his fury at the device. With the knife stuck in the forcefield, the bot couldn't turn to aim at him. Terry thought that was weird, but appreciated that it couldn't kill him while he was killing it.

He drove the bot downward. It tried to fly away, but it wasn't strong enough to fly while the big human was attached to it, so Terry rammed it into the wall. The energy shield acted as a damper, protecting it from being pinned. When the Ka-bar's point reached the metal, Terry slid it until it caught one of the many seams, then he ripped with barbaric vigor, driving the point deeper into the metal construct.

When he hit something important, the end came quickly. The shield disappeared, and the propulsion ceased; it dropped like a bowling ball. Terry followed it to the floor. He wasn't sure it was dead, but pulled his knife free and stabbed it into the orifice from which its laser had fired. With a cracked crystal, if it came back to life, it wouldn't be shooting at them.

Terry hurried back to Char. Her face was a mess; the flesh was torn and shredded, and one eye was swollen shut. He cradled her to his chest, but the raw hamburger that was his stomach added his blood to hers.

He rocked her, feeling her pulse beneath his fingers and trusting the nanocytes to do their job and repair their injuries. Terry listened, hoping that another bot wasn't on its way, but he could hear nothing besides his own blood pounding in his ears. The skin on his arms was bright red and had started to bubble.

"*Gott Verdammt*, TH!" Bethany Anne bitched. She stood wearing her glossy black armor and a look of concern. "I can't leave you two for a minute."

"I'd prefer that you didn't leave us at all," Terry replied.

"I don't seem to have any control over that," BA admitted. "I'm here now, though. What do you need me to do?"

"Find a control room where we can summon the elevator, or I'd settle for a stairway if such a thing wasn't too backward for the Kurtherians."

The Queen turned and strode down the hallway, her mid-calf boots with extended heels not making a sound. She stopped at a four-way intersection about seventy-five meters down the corridor, where she looked in each direction before taking a left and disappearing from sight around the corner.

"Always turn left and you won't get lost," he said after her.

Terry felt exhausted. He'd been seriously injured three times in the course of thirty minutes. Char's features were coming back together, but she was still dead to the world. Terry closed his eyes for just a moment, and that was all he remembered.

When Terry woke, the lights were off. Char was in his arms, breathing slowly and deeply as she always did when she slept.

"Bethany Anne?" he called, but she didn't answer.

Char stirred and mumbled, "I feel like shit."

"We've covered no ground and almost been killed twice by relics from a zillion years ago. This isn't cutting-edge Kurtherian tech. These are the long-forgotten castoffs, and they are as deadly now as they were back then."

Char sat up and carefully stroked the new skin of her face. "Got your flashlight handy?"

He pulled it out and turned it on. He smiled. "Beautiful as ever." He touched her face and changed the angle of the light. "All healed. How long were we out?"

"At least an hour?" Char guessed. Together they stood, then Char found her flashlight and added its light to Terry's. "Anything new?"

"I think we're fine, but we need to start making progress."

"It's a puzzle box," Char suggested. "We get lights, security bots, forcefields, and elevators, and it's all interconnected. We get one thing to do what we want, and something else happens."

"Lights don't mean security. It's the opposite. And the weapons made us a target." Terry started to pace. "How about we try opening a door but not going in?"

"I'm good with anything that doesn't blow up in my face." She turned off her flashlight to save power.

Terry walked past the room with shielded boxes. This time, it didn't open when he waved his hand in front of the activation pad. "What the fuck?" he grumbled and stopped. The wreckage of the security bot remained on the floor. "Visual or wireless?"

"As in, does this thing open doors and turn on lights because of how it looks, or from the data it exchanges with the mothership?"

"My guess would be the latter, but let's take it with us." Terry's coat was shredded and covered in dried blood. Before he picked up the robot, he checked his pockets. One of his water containers had been punctured, and the circuit board from the other bot had been shattered. "Shit."

"I'm sorry, Terry." Char gripped his arm to stop him from continuing down the corridor.

"Don't be, lover. I know. I'm the hardest guy ever to buy a present for." He kissed her. "Thank you for trying to make this special for me. I owe you a pair of Louboutin boots. Thinking about things that are needed, maybe the universe could use a *Westworld*-type amusement park. Escape from the Kurtherians."

"All we need to do is escape first," Char suggested.

"Puzzle box. This is an escape room, but it's real," Terry declared.

"An escape room has an exit and isn't trying to kill you."

"Details, details!" Terry laughed lightly as the situation gelled within his mind to something that made sense. A problem to figure out instead of something he had to fight his way through, even though he needed to do that, too. He killed a security bot with his Ka-bar.

"The devil's in the details," Bethany Anne's voice came from the darkness.

"Welcome back, BA. Did you find anything?" Terry asked.

"I found a couple of Etheric power sources that are lighting up the universe. Everyone should be able to see us down here now."

"A door slammed shut as the elevator came down the shaft. I think it's shielded again. All that power is being used to hide all that power."

BA walked to the wall and turned toward them. "This is a bunch of shit. Can't you two party like normal people?"

Char shook her head. "We're not normal people. None of us."

BA didn't reply, just leaned casually against the wall and waited.

"This is more like how we party. Let's rip the fabric of the universe so we can make stuffed animals to give out to children!" Terry quipped, shining his flashlight down the corridor to make sure nothing was trying to sneak up on them. "Can we get to the power supplies? Do you know what would happen if we shut them down?"

"How the hell would I know? That's TOM and ADAM's job. They have to earn their fucking keep somehow, and at the moment, those two miscreants are AWOL. Not exactly going to get glowing marks on their next HR reports."

It made sense. "She's right."

"Which means that none of us know. How can we find out without killing ourselves?"

"There's the million-credit question," Bethany Anne remarked. "Follow me, and let's take a look. We sure as hell can't find out what it will do from here."

BA started to walk but fast, more like a trot. Terry and Char had to run to keep up. The Queen turned left at a four-way intersection, the same way she had gone last time they saw her.

Terry didn't want to lose her. Every other time she had disappeared, the Kurtherians had taken out their vengeance on Terry and Char, tripping the traps set untold ages ago.

They hurried past numerous doorways and a few connecting passages. The space between doors grew until they took another left, branching off the main corridor that widened as it disappeared into the distance.

"Looks like a survival shelter. Why didn't they come down here when the city above was getting attacked?" Terry asked.

"Looks like something out of *Stargate*. I expect to see the gate room through one of these doors."

"Fuck!" Terry waved the beam of his flashlight across the corridor ahead. He hugged the remainder of the bot with his other arm and shook his head, his flashlight turned behind them and then forward once more. "She's gone again."

Char stiffened.

Before they could move, the lights came on.

CHAPTER SIX

<u>Efluyez Homeworld, Alganor Sector</u>

The *War Axe* settled into orbit and waited for clearance to land. Micky watched the screen, counting the number and types of ships.

"Freighters, container ships, bulk liquid carriers," he intoned. "Four warships that are nothing more than police vessels."

He sighed heavily and rested his head on his hand, trying not to look bored.

"Flayse Control to the *War Axe*. Welcome! It is a great day for all Flayse, seeing your magnificence in orbit!"

Micky choked back a snort before opening the channel. "Thank you for the warm welcome, Flayse Control. Please give us clearance and coordinates, and we'll begin our descent to your lovely planet."

There was a long delay. Micky pursed his lips. "Smedley?"

Before the AI could answer, the planet replied.

"That won't be possible. There is simply nowhere for

such a great ship to rest at ease. If you could send your people down in shuttles, we'll be ready to receive them."

Christina held up a finger to Micky, then drew it across her throat.

"Channel closed," the skipper announced.

"Fuck that," Christina stated. "This is starting to stink like a massive setup. Open the channel."

Smedley acknowledged, and the captain waited with bated breath for Christina to deliver a dose of reality to the Flayse.

"This Colonel Christina Lowell. I'm in charge of the Bad Company, and if we can't bring the *War Axe* with us, we're not going to come. Our Pods create an unacceptable vulnerability as we divide our force among non-combatant vessels."

The Pods were shielded and built to withstand ground fire, but she didn't need to tell them that.

"We cannot change the fact that there is nowhere for your ship to land," Flayse Control insisted. "That is a mighty big ship you have. Please send your shuttles. We are waiting."

"We're going back home now. Good luck with your parade." Christina had Smedley close the channel. "Take us out of orbit and prepare to Gate us the fuck out of here."

The *War Axe* turned and slowly accelerated away from Efluyez.

Smedley interrupted the exodus, as Christina and Micky had expected.

"Flayse Control is demonstrating a certain amount of cognitive dissonance in their wailing and gnashing of teeth."

"Have they rent their clothing?" Christina asked, demonstrating her classical and broad education.

"Torn their clothing? I have no idea," the AI replied evenly.

"Open the channel."

"...please come back!" Flayse Control pleaded.

"Listen here, you mealy-mouthed piece of shit. Stop jacking me around. You know we don't have to land, so we can put the *War Axe* anywhere. How about you go fuck yourself!" Christina's knuckles were white on the fist she was shaking at the image of the planet. "I want to speak with the head of the conglomerate. The one we signed the contract with, not you, you fucking lackey."

Smedley cut the connection.

"A little harsh, don't you think?" Micky asked.

"I guess if you're the lackey following orders, then maybe it was. Sorry, lackey," she told the screen even though communication with Flayse Control had been terminated.

"I have the office of the Magnate requesting to speak with Colonel Lowell."

"How long did that take, Smedley?"

"From closed channel to open channel, it was exactly twenty-eight seconds."

"Lackey has some chops to get that kind of response."

"Shall I turn the ship back toward the planet?"

Christina turned to Micky and he gestured back, deferring the decision. "Activate the Gate drive, but don't take us through. First, open a channel to Flayse Control."

The engine spooled up and the Gate appeared, the event horizon beckoning.

"Channel open."

"Flayse Control, this is Colonel Lowell. Please accept my apologies. Name-calling was wholly unacceptable. Thank you for notifying the office of the Magnate."

"No need to apologize for my rudeness, Colonel. Does that mean you're going to start sending your shuttles down?"

Christina looked at the ceiling before killing the channel. "Fuckwit."

"What if he has a gun to his head?"

"Then he's going to have a real bad day, and serving up the *War Axe* on the altar of malfeasance would cost other people their lives. We should probably turn this whole planet over to the Magistrates and let them clean up this little cesspool."

"Are you sure it's a cesspool?" Micky asked.

"The Magnate is waiting," Smedley interrupted.

"They appear to want to control us as part of their intimidation tactics. I won't sell out the Bad Company like that. My dad will be pissed if I make his company look like a bunch of toads."

"I agree. We can't put your people at risk. Where am I going to find another Bad Company to put on board? You have the best parties. Jenelope would be mad if I got you all killed."

"Wenceslaus too, I imagine," Christina replied before twirling her finger in the air. "Let me talk with the Magnate."

"Colonel Lowell? Colonel Lowell of the Bad Company, please respond," a disembodied voice requested.

"There you are!" Christina declared. "This is Colonel Lowell."

"I am the secretary of the Magnate, and it appears there has been a minor misunderstanding." A male-sounding voice dripped the syrupy words.

Christina turned to Micky and mouthed the word "lackey."

"We will be more than happy," the voice continued, "to provide a ship to shuttle your people to the surface of Efluyez."

"Please put the Magnate on. You have one minute before we fly through the Gate, never to return to Efluyez."

"There is no need to get the Magnate involved with the logistics of your presence."

"You are correct. Please notify your Magnate of your failure in misleading us. *War Axe*, out."

"WAIT!" the voice both cried and pleaded with the single word. "I'm transmitting your landing coordinates now. Please don't run into anything on your way down." The communication disconnected.

"That wasn't so hard, was it? Fucking asswipes. Major Kimber!" Christina talked to the ceiling as Terry Henry did when communicating with and through Smedley. "Put four people into their mechanized combat suits. I don't trust these jack-wagons one bit. I don't know what their game is, but I'm not playing. I want armor support at all times while we're on the planet. No one wanders off by themselves."

"Roger that, Colonel. These people are giving me a case of the willies."

"I have the coordinates. Begin descent?" Clifton asked

from the pilot's chair. Christina gave him a thumbs-up before she headed off the bridge.

"Let's see what kind of surprise we can deliver to our *gracious* hosts," she mumbled to herself.

Abandoned Kurtherian Outpost, Okkoto, the Fourth Moon Orbiting Cygnus VI

Terry backed against the wall, and Char stood behind him. "How long are you going to hang on to that bot?"

"I killed it with a knife. It's my only source of pride out of this whole debacle. I want to mount it and put it on the wall," Terry joked, his voice tense with expectation of the unknown.

"The plan is to do nothing," Char stated, making it sound like a question.

"We have not yet tried it, and nothing else seems to be working."

Char didn't correct him. Everything they had tried had worked against them.

The faint sound of another bot came to them from farther down the corridor. Terry had to force his breathing to slow.

A security bot hovered into view. Similar to the one that Terry carried in his arm, it stopped and moved slowly back and forth across the corridor. After what seemed like forever but was probably only a few moments, the bot continued toward them. It stopped again once it reached the humans, moved back and forth and up and down, and gave them a good scan before bumping into the other bot.

Terry let go a little at a time to make sure it didn't fall.

The other bot extended its propulsion system, and together, the two bots headed down the hallway.

"Easy come," Terry started. The new bot stopped and twisted violently around. It fired, but Terry and Char were already running. They cleared the corner of the intersection with Char going right and Terry left. He pulled his combat knife and prepared to attack.

He waited, listening for the bot's approach. Char cupped a hand around her ear before shaking her head. She couldn't hear anything. They waited a couple minutes, barely breathing to avoid missing it. The lights went out.

Terry turned on his flashlight and shined it down the empty corridor. "It doesn't like us talking. Speaking English is enough to have us killed, but not worth running after us to do the deed. Who programmed this shit?"

"Stupid Kurtherians? Castoffs?"

"I don't think it was their A-Team, but that makes them more dangerous because they're less predictable."

"We stand still, let them do their thing, and then move on. I think our odds are improving," Char suggested.

"We gained a laser pistol and then lost it. We gained a security bot and then lost it. We arrived in an elevator and then lost it. I think the Kurtherians are bullying us, and it's starting to piss me off!"

"That's the spirit!" Char cheered, her face a perfect mask of insincerity.

Terry wasn't sure if he wanted to fight about it, but his whining was getting them no closer to the surface.

"Keep going this way? Now that the threat is gone, I expect Bethany Anne to show up. Maybe she'll be able to show us what she found."

Char started walking, and Terry joined her. He stopped to examine the scorch mark on the wall. The security bot had not been a figment of his imagination. There was a long stretch of about one hundred meters that had no doors. It was only an empty corridor.

"Was this an afterthought? Maybe a connector to a different part of the complex?" Terry mused.

Char used her flashlight to check the walls. "They seem to be made from the same material as the other corridors."

Terry strode boldly to the end before stopping to peek around the corner. He had to shine the flashlight into the darkness to see what was beyond.

"Lots of doors." He leaned against the wall for a span before taking a second look. "If I didn't know better, I'd say it was a dormitory. If we could get in one of the rooms, we would know for sure. There's a room for security bots and a power station at the very least."

"Down here," Bethany Anne called from the darkness. Terry shined his light on her. "Get that bloody llama-licking light out of my face!"

Terry directed it to the floor and looked knowingly at Char before following the oft-absent Queen to the end of the hallway.

"I'm thinking this is a barracks or dormitory of sorts."

"I agree, TH. There's nothing in these rooms."

"How did you get in?" Terry asked, trusting her, but still wanting to see for himself.

"I don't know. I just did. This is really pissing me off." She waved a hand in front of doors as she passed. Terry and Char followed her lead, but none of them opened until they reached the end. "Here it is. The Etheric power station."

BA stepped aside. Terry didn't hesitate. He strode to the door, and it opened without him having to stop. He walked through, confident that BA wouldn't send him into a trap.

He stopped once inside when his flashlight beam showed a man—a seemingly human man.

"Ah," the being said. "I need a hand, if you'd be a sport."

"Who are you?" Terry blurted.

"Tonie Sall-mon. And you?"

"I'm Terry Henry Walton," TH replied without thinking.

"May I call you Terry? Right! Put your finger here and hold that down while I make some adjustments over there." He pointed in the general direction of an equipment stand.

"Right!" Terry replied mockingly, not moving to help.

"Chop-chop! You want the lights on, don't you?"

"How in the fuck do you know that?"

Char leaned around her husband and shined her light into the rest of the room, looking for any other surprises. She saw a place that looked like the engine room on Ted's ship, *Ramses' Chariot*.

"What kind of holographic hell have we fallen into?" Char wondered.

Bethany Anne walked around TH and went straight for Tonie.

"You're still here," Terry said, pleasantly surprised.

She dialed up her middle finger and held it behind her back while she addressed Tonie.

"What's going to happen when he presses that button?" BA swiped her arm through the being, confirming Char's observation. "A hologram."

"I may be, or I may not be." He shook his head. "Usually, every group has a smart one, but I'm beginning to wonder about you three."

"Where is the computer that's driving you?"

Tonie shrugged. "Are we going to turn on the lights or not?"

"What is all of this?" BA asked, pointing at the door and waving her hand to take in the entire complex.

"This place is called Band Rayal Seven. This is the fallout shelter. We've been at war so long that every one of our towns is built only after the shelter is in place."

"'Band Rayal?' I have never heard of that Kurtherian name." BA put her hands on her hips and stared at Tonie in disbelief.

"I don't know what a Kurtherian is, but I'm pretty sure I'm not one."

"When did they start using the word 'Kurtherian' to describe themselves?" Terry wondered. He dug deep into his memory, but he had never bothered learning what there was to know about the elder alien race. "Haven't they ascended? Who is this guy?"

"I'm Tonie," the being insisted. "I belong to a race called the 'Erthos.'"

"Erthosian?" Terry asked.

"No."

Terry waved impatiently at the abrupt answer. "We're trapped down here and want out. How do we get back to the surface?"

"Yes, right! If you're down here, then the pathways are open. How have my people evolved? I am curious. You look like fine specimens."

"The city up top was blasted to rubble eons ago. No one knew this place existed. I fear that no one has looked for survivors down here in a *very* long time. And we're not your people. We're from Earth."

"Earth. That is what we Erthos would have called one of our seed planets. Can you give the star reference?" TH shook his head. "No? That is most upsetting," Tonie said, his face turning dark for a couple heartbeats before he shook it off and brightened. "Right! Finger." He pointed to the panel.

BA nodded and Terry did as he was told. He pressed the button. Tonie went to work on the cabinet before him that started to flash and hum.

"How long do I..." Terry started to ask, but he stopped when the lights came on and Tonie cheered in triumph.

"And there we are, one step closer to returning our little corner of the world to a fully functioning shelter."

"You mean to say, 'a fully functioning shelter with access for the humans to come and go as they please,'" BA corrected.

"I don't know about all that. These shelters were meant to be self-sufficient. However, since you're down here, it must mean that the access shafts have opened."

"Shaft-*s*." Char emphasized the plural. "Please point them out to us."

"I don't have a screen in here."

"Display one using your holographic projectors!" Terry commanded.

Tonie looked at the human as if he'd sprung a second head.

"Go back the way you came, through the dormitory,

take a right at the T intersection, then another right at the four-way. Follow it straight all the way to the end, then take a left. The main elevator is there. It'll deliver you to the Consul General's building."

"What language are you speaking? All your terms are the same as ours," Terry wondered.

"I'm speaking what you best understand."

Terry tapped his temple as if that would help his chip. He couldn't tell if the entity was speaking English or if it was getting translated. From what Terry could see, the lips moved in sync with the words he heard.

Char twisted her head back and forth to see if it made a difference and shook her head. She couldn't tell either.

"We know about that one. It's the one we used to come down here."

"Then take it back up," Tonie replied.

"The doors won't open for us." Terry crossed his arms and scowled. A person with all the information was standing right in front of them, yet he couldn't tell them anything.

"That *is* a problem." Tonie thought about it for a moment before talking again. "Go to the first T and take a left, and follow that down, staying to the left, until you come to a dead end. That last door is a staircase, but it is heavily protected. If you couldn't get through an elevator door, I doubt you'll make it to the stairway."

"We would love to take the elevator," Bethany Anne interjected. "Can you open the doors for us before I become annoyed enough to pull your lungs out through your ass to encourage better relations?"

Tonie stared at the violent woman. "That's a built-in

security feature. I cannot override it. I don't have sufficient rank to do that."

"I suggest," Terry said, "that since you are the only one 'alive' down here, you are all things, including governor, president, and Grand Poobah. You name it, you're it. Give yourself the clearance and make the magic happen. All you have to do is believe in yourself."

Terry smiled broadly and gestured for Tonie to get to it.

"It takes more than believing in myself. It takes access, which I don't have in order to give myself access. You see, as much as you'd like to build up my confidence, which I greatly appreciate regardless, we have an irresolvable dichotomy."

"Hack the system. No one is here to stop you. And since we're in Federation space, I can have my dad authorize it, so you can't get in trouble," Bethany Anne stated.

"Oh." Tonie shook his head. "I can't do that."

"As useless as tits on a boar hog." BA crossed her arms and glared.

"At least the lights are on." Char turned her head toward Tonie. "Can you make it so we can enter the common rooms?"

"Anyone should be able to," Tonie replied before changing his mind and saying, "Take this. It'll let you in."

He undid his wristband and tossed it. Terry caught it. He expected it to be a hologram. "This is solid."

"Of course, it's solid. It's my access band."

Terry and Char looked at him, stupefied by the revelation that the hologram wore a real wristband.

"What do you say we check on that stairwell?" Terry asked BA.

The Queen turned to Char and lifted her eyebrows in question.

"So say we all," Char declared. BA smiled and nodded, motioning for Terry to go first. He strolled through and held the door. After Char passed through, Terry looked back into the power room. Tonie was fussing around with the equipment, while BA was nowhere to be seen.

"Where did she go?" Terry asked.

"Who?" The being's answer left Terry wondering about his own sanity.

CHAPTER SEVEN

The *War Axe* dominated the landscape, hovering above the parade ground where all of those marching would congregate. Four days remained until they could do their thing and leave.

Christina ran out the front of the hangar and leapt, dropping the ten meters to the ground. A number of warriors joined her, Kimber, Kai, Joseph, and Petricia. Aaron and Yanmei waited deep within the hangar bay inside the cockpits of the Black Eagles in case they were needed. They could launch in seconds if they received the call.

They watched the meeting between Christina and the Flayse Conglomerate on their screens while Micky did the same thing from the bridge. Wenceslaus, the big orange cat, had found his way in and was sleeping on the captain's lap. Micky stroked his fur absentmindedly as he watched for the subterfuge they all expected.

A cloud of cat hair drifted away from his fingers as he

kept petting the cat, and a circle of hair started to form on his uniform trousers. Wenceslaus purred loudly.

Outside, the five warriors avoided bunching together. Their heads swiveled back and forth as their eyes sought the threats they were sure were there. Joseph focused on what he could see in their minds. Two mech-suited warriors clumped to the hangar bay door and stood, menacing the area. Above, the *War Axe*'s weaponry moved back and forth to let the aliens know that their deaths were only a heartbeat away if they wanted to take a shot at the Bad Company.

Minions, Joseph told the group.

The first one who approached put both hands to his chest and bowed. "I am the Magnate's Executive Secretary. I am to handle all of your concerns and make you feel welcome while also confirming that you are appropriately intimidating."

Christina planted her fists on her hips and glared at the secretary until he averted his eyes.

"You'll do," he said softly.

"I'm Colonel Christina Lowell. My deputy, Major Kimber, and Kai, Joseph, and Petricia. Can you show us where we'll form up, and the route we'll march?"

"Yes, but you'll have to move that abomination." The secretary gestured toward the ship hovering nearby.

Rise five hundred meters and take a position another thousand to the south, Christina ordered.

"That *abomination* is an intelligent ship, one of the most powerful in the galaxy. It's also my home. I'll ask you to hold your insubordinate tongue."

"Of course, Liege Master." The secretary cowered with his head bowed.

They said they were passive. Is that what it looks like? Passive-aggressive? Or are they just a bunch of dicks who people want to beat up? It would be a lot cheaper if they were nicer, Kimber suggested.

Christina clenched her jaw to keep the laugh from escaping and sent a warning glance toward Kimber, who assumed a look of innocence.

Kai winked.

Joseph's brow wrinkled as he focused on the secretary.

Ask him about the Frikandans, Joseph requested.

The *War Axe* moved to its new position and faced the parade deck. The group started walking away from a viewing area that was already set up, complete with royal bunting and massive flags flowing overhead.

"Mister Secretary, according to our contract, we're here to show your neighbors that you mean business. Tell me about Frikanda and its people."

He made faces as if he'd eaten a chili-dipped bug.

"Never mind," Christina conceded, clapping the secretary on the back. Joseph nodded slowly before sharing what he learned.

They want to leverage us to start a war with Frikanda that we then fight for them. They want us not to intimidate their neighbors but eliminate them as a threat, a competitor, and fellow residents of this system.

Genocide? Christina wondered.

Just short of that. Kill any Frikandan who can hold a weapon.

Christina stopped the secretary. "This is far enough. I

can see everything we need to see. Form up over there and march to that corner, then that corner." The colonel pointed as she talked her way through the parade route. "Will there be anyone else in the parade?"

"No. You *are* the parade," the secretary confirmed.

"That's fine. We were prepared for that. We'll need to leave the second the parade is over. If you need us for anything after that, we'll have to negotiate a new contract."

The man's eyes shot wide in panic before he could steel his expression.

Why didn't they want the War Axe *down here if they wanted us to start a war?* Christina asked.

Maybe the Frikandans won't come if we're on the surface in force, Kimber replied. *They'll wait for us to leave before attacking, which would gain the Flayse nothing.*

The assassination of Archduke Ferdinand, Christina replied. *The catalyst to start a world war back on Earth. The Flayse are planning to kill one of us and blame their neighbors.*

Sounds more like The Princess Bride. *I love that movie!* Kai interrupted.

"Thank you, Mister Secretary." Christina inclined her head slightly. "We'll be on our way now, and will return in three days. We have some business we need to conduct with the Frikandans. Bye!"

She made a show of turning her back and hurrying away from their sputtering escort.

Band Rayal Seven, Okkoto

Terry waved his access bracelet at every door as he

passed. One finally opened and he started to go in, but Char stopped him.

He didn't understand.

"This is probably Tonie's room. We shouldn't abuse the access he gave us."

"Tonie has been dead for a million years, give or take. He's a hologram," Terry tried to explain, but his words rang hollow. He looked at the bracelet on his wrist.

Char saw him look at it. "Why does a hologram have a real wristband?"

"He had it when he passed. Maybe their holographic technology is so advanced that it projects a solid object?" Terry offered.

"BA put her hand through him. He's a hologram."

"With a real wristband," Terry muttered, talking himself in a circle. "I have to look."

Char let him go, resigning herself to looking at the room from the doorway. The door remained open while she blocked it with her body.

She glanced back down the corridor to confirm that no one was there—not a security bot, not Bethany Anne.

Terry checked the small room, the drawers, and the small, immersive entertainment area. There was a minimalist recliner with holo-emitters, but no desk or other chairs. A small bed and an integrated bathroom rounded out the room. The drawers contained utilitarian clothing. There were no personal effects that Terry could find.

"We could fit if we have to sleep here," Terry said. He wasn't trying to be cute. He had shifted from being skeptical about the experience to embracing survival mode.

"There has to be a separate kitchen. There is no food or water in here."

Char internalized Terry's observations. It was everything she had expected.

"Your wristband should open the door to the chow hall or any other community space," Char reiterated.

"And therein lies the can of worms. What lies within?" Terry intoned, humorlessly. "Let's see what kinds of defenses are around the stairwell."

"Can we check the wristband to see if it will summon the elevator?" Char asked.

"I like the way you think. Time to get out of here."

He strolled away, carrying nothing but whatever his shredded coat could handle. Char's coat didn't look much better.

"How long has it been since we came down here?" Char asked.

"I wish I knew." The chips in their heads were for translation and communication. Without being linked to Smedley or another system, there was nothing for the chip to share. "I never wanted this thing in my head, but then it turned out to be useful, so we did away with things like watches. Now that we're disconnected, I would appreciate something as simple as a wind-up wristwatch."

When Terry and Char reached the first corner, they stopped and peeked around it. They didn't have to expose themselves for long with the lights on. A quick duck into the open and back revealed all the corridor's secrets. They continued to the T intersection, and then to the four-way intersection, where they walked briskly straight ahead. A door on the left opened as they passed.

Terry jumped back, thrusting Char behind him, and the door closed. He stepped closer and waved his arm at it, and the automatic system responded. Inside, tables with chairs were arranged in a similar way to the mess deck on the *War Axe*.

One occupant sat, enjoying what the system had to offer. Bethany Anne had a huge bowl in front of her and a spoon the size of a ladle. "Banana split," she mumbled around a mouthful of ice cream."

"How do the Erthos have banana splits? Wasn't that invented in Latrobe?" Terry wondered.

"Ice cream!" Char exclaimed. BA patted the seat next to her.

"How does it work?"

Bethany Anne pointed to a wall where a stainless steel door was recessed.

"Tell that thing what you want, and it appears."

"What if it's poisonous?" Terry asked.

"I thought your nanos were tougher than that? What's a little poison?" BA rationalized with a half-shrug. "It's the other white meat."

Terry had no comeback. Char ordered a banana split, and a light appeared inside the device a moment later. Char reached in and pulled out her ice cream, tasted it, and hummed with delight. Terry gave in to his hunger.

"A triple hamburger with cheese, extra pickles, and French fries, please."

He removed his meal. "How in the hell did it know what all that was?" he asked, showing the plate to the women. The Queen pointed to the chair opposite hers.

Terry walked around the table to sit where she had

directed. He took a bite, savoring it as he chewed. "We'll need this recipe for my All Guns Blazing."

"You have an All Guns Blazing?" Bethany Anne asked.

"It's a franchise, but yes. On Keeg Station in the Dren Cluster where we set up the Bad Company's Direct Action Branch."

"Terry Henry Walton owns a brewery," BA stated. "I guess it was inevitable. Is Nathan paying you too much?"

Nathan Lowell was BA's long-time friend and the president of the Bad Company.

"That wasn't it," Char said between bites. "There was a massive bet, a series of lines on how long TH could go without swearing. He beat them all, especially Nathan and your father."

"I'll be damned. My dad and Nathan financed your bar. When I get to talk to Dad again, I'll have to bust him on the lost bet."

Terry shook his head because he'd taken a big enough bite that he couldn't speak. When he finally swallowed, he said, "Don't be fooled by what you're eating. All of this stuff is a million years old."

BA shrugged. "So what? It tastes good right now. Don't try to rub the shine off this ice cream sundae."

The door opened, and a person dressed like Tonie walked in. She stopped when she saw the three humans but didn't say anything. Four more Erthos followed her in, nearly running into her. They spread out to look at BA and company.

Terry stood and turned since he had sat with his back to the door, then smiled and waved. "I'm Terry Henry

Walton, and my compliments to your chef. This is the best burger I've had in forever."

The five didn't change expression.

A sixth person entered the room, walking to the side of the others. She looked different and dressed differently, her expression more severe and her hair tight against her head. "We don't often get strangers," she said softly, glaring without blinking.

"How often is not too often?" Terry asked.

"I was being kind. We *never* get strangers. For you to be here, something very bad must have happened. We need to find out what it was." She finally took her eyes off the humans and looked at the other Erthos. "Seize them."

"Fuck that!" Bethany Anne leapt over the table and headed for the far end of the line. Terry dove across the tables to take out the three Erthos in the middle. Char rushed around her toward the one giving the orders.

Terry caught sight of Bethany Anne executing a series of roundhouse kicks and throat punches, but she didn't seem to be connecting. She laughed as the Erthos backed slowly away from her.

Terry had three of them before him. He lashed out with a front kick and sent that Erthos through the door and into the wall beyond. Two aliens tried to grab Terry's arms and he let them, then spun them so their backs were to him. He secured both in headlocks and started to squeeze.

Char squared off against the Erthos female, who crossed her arms and threw her shoulders back. When Char punched her in the mouth, she staggered, her arms fell limp to her side, and she went down. The next man swung a roundhouse at Char.

She lunged forward, caught his wild swing under her left arm, and rotated toward him, delivering an elbow strike between his eyes. His head snapped back and he dropped, slamming the back of his melon into the hard floor, where he lay still. Char wondered if he was dead. She spared an extra moment to look at him since Terry had his targets under control.

After a final flex, Terry dropped the two unconscious forms. BA was standing to the side while her opponent cowered against the wall.

"I'll beat this dickwad using only my mind," she remarked. Terry grabbed the last one standing and propelled him into a chair.

"How the hell do we get out of here?" Terry demanded.

"I don't know," the male stammered.

"I'm about out of patience with the I-don't-know answers I'm getting down here. How about an easier one. How long have you lived here?"

"My whole life. All of us have, like our parents before us."

"You look like a work detail. Where did you come from?"

"Work. We maintain Air Handling System Four and Hydroponics Bay Seven."

"Four and seven? There are seven hydroponics bays?"

"There are twelve." He didn't come across as wanting to hide anything.

"What's your name, son?" Terry said, taking a seat next to the Erthos.

"I am Zayn Tova."

"Nice to meet you." Terry offered his hand but Zayn

backed away, glancing at the floor where the four bodies of his fellows remained unmoving. The door had closed, and his fifth companion was outside in the corridor. Terry put his hands to his chest and bowed as he'd seen Tonie do.

The alien responded in kind.

Bethany Anne interrupted, "I might be older, but I'm not necessarily more patient. So, now that we're all friends, why don't you show us where all the people are?"

"I'm afraid there aren't that many," he mumbled toward the floor.

BA nodded, having already read his body language and understanding what the man was holding back.

"Go," she told him. Terry's head snapped to her. "We have all we need."

The Erthos rose and walked quickly from the dining area. When the door popped open, the body in the hallway was still crumpled in a pile.

"Check them. I expect you'll find they are all dead."

Terry and Char went about the grim business to confirm what BA suspected. "Why?"

"Remnants of the civilization left behind. They have devolved to the point where they are satisfied by merely existing."

"No different from cattle."

"But no one is eating this lot. When one dies, they make another one."

"Clones?"

"Illegal in my Federation, but without cloning, there would be no Erthos."

"But the lights. Why weren't the lights on?"

"It was their night?" Bethany Anne suggested. "Lights are on because it's daytime now.

Terry removed a wristband from one of the dead and offered it to BA. She shook her head.

"No need. Give it to your lovely bride."

He handed it to Char.

"I *knew* you had a crush," Char quipped.

"What?" Terry held his hand to his chest in shock. "Neither in thought nor deed have I crushed on anyone else."

He smiled innocently.

BA rolled her eyes as Char scowled, and BA pointed at the purple-eyed werewolf. "Oh, no. He's *your* boy scout. Loyal as a Golden Retriever, but he has horrendous taste in movies, although the music I'm good with." She paused for a moment. "How can you stand it?"

"What's wrong with the movies I like?"

Char and Bethany Anne laughed at a joke only they understood. Terry searched the Erthos who looked different from the others, the one who was in charge. She carried nothing, just like the others, but Terry took her band and handed it to Char.

"Let's check that elevator. The express train out of here might let us on board."

Charumati held Terry back and pulled him to her. "I'm ready to get out of here." She kissed him fiercely. When they separated, Bethany Anne's face was inches from theirs. They leaned away.

"Are we ready to go yet? Michael is probably wondering where I am. I'll have to tell him that I was tortured by you two engaging in intramural tonsil tickling.

Come on!" She clapped her hands, but it made no sound. "Places to go, people to see."

Terry and Char stepped over the bodies and into the hall. The one that had been there was gone, and Zayn was nowhere to be seen either. "I suspect that when we return, there won't be any bodies in the chow hall, either."

"Judging by the lack of dust in this place, they recycle every speck. BA?" Char turned back.

BA gestured toward the hall. "I need to check on something here. I'll be along in a bit."

Terry looked askance. "More ice cream with your name on it?"

"They interrupted my breakfast," she deadpanned.

Terry waved, and they continued toward the elevator. When they arrived, they found the door closed. Terry waved his wristband at it, but nothing happened. Char waved her two wristbands, and the door opened.

"Woohoo!" Terry cheered and pumped a fist. They climbed aboard and waited. Finally, Terry tried something. "Take us to the surface."

"Take us up," Char offered. "Surface. Ground floor. Up. Anywhere other than here..."

Terry dug through the remaining pockets of his jacket and found a small first aid kit. He pulled it apart to wedge the pieces into the door, something he hadn't done last time. Char looked it over and pulled on the gauze packed under the tight-fitting door. She couldn't budge it.

"That should work."

"Bets that BA and the bodies are both gone when we get back?" Terry asked.

"Now I'm curious, but I know you're right. This place is

creeping me out," Char said softly. "Too much weird shit. We don't see anyone, then there's a thriving community. BA is here, and then she's not. The food was too good to be true, and exactly what we wanted."

She grabbed the skin on the back of her husband's hand and twisted. He grimaced and rubbed the spot. "What the hell was that all about?"

"I think we're dreaming. We're living *Total Recall* or some bullshit."

"Like fuck we are," Terry countered. "I died twice in here, and you once. That hurt enough for me to know it was real. This isn't a dream, but I'm beginning to form a hypothesis."

They started walking and after they turned the corner. Terry held a finger to his lips and crept back to the wall's edge. He peeked around to find the elevator door open, exactly as they left it.

"Looking good so far," he allowed. When they made it back to the cafeteria, Char waved her band and the door opened, showing them it was empty inside.

"Staircase?"

"My thoughts exactly." Terry strode away with Char by his side.

CHAPTER EIGHT

The *War Axe* orbiting the Efluyez Homeworld, Alganor Sector

"What if they don't pay us?" Kimber asked.

Christina looked out the front of the hangar bay at the stars beyond the Alganor system. "Then we'll still be alive."

"Do you think they can hurt us?" Kimber shifted her feet and turned to Joseph.

"I believe they can. Their thoughts are guarded well, but Christina's premise of an attack on the Bad Company being a catalyst to galvanize us into action is sound. It makes the most sense from what I saw."

"Looks like we're marching in a parade," Christina said.

"You just said it was a trap." Kimber was confused.

"But we know it's a trap, so that way we can avoid it."

"By marching right into it."

"Exactly," Christina agreed, slapping her deputy on the shoulder. "Follow me. We have some work to do."

"Aren't we going to Frikanda?"

"We'll do a flyby so we can collect information on their

forces and give these knotheads the impression that we've met with their enemies. All the while, we'll be figuring out how to foil an ambush from within the kill zone."

Band Rayal Seven, Okkoto

"Where did you go?" Terry asked the missing corpses. He leaned down to study the floor and shined his flashlight across the surface, letting the shadows of anything remaining give him clues. "Look."

Terry pointed to a small line—not dust, but a thread from clothing.

"And another." It was like a trail of breadcrumbs. Only two, but it showed him the way. "There's an access port here, like a Roomba hole."

Char started shaking her head. "I know what you're thinking."

"*I* don't even know what I'm thinking, but maybe if you share, I can think it with you."

"I'm not going in there."

"Hell! I wasn't thinking that, but I should have. It's a great idea!" Terry blurted as he pushed on the door to find that it was double-hinged even though it settled into the wall without a telltale line showing its presence. Terry didn't wait for Char's rebuttal, just dropped to his belly and pulled himself in. His bulging coat remnants caught on the frame, and he pushed himself back out.

"What are you doing?" Char asked when Terry took off his coat. He rifled the pockets to remove the things he needed—protein bars, one remaining pouch of water, multi-tool, and the flashlight.

"I expect it'll be gone when we return."

"I don't want to go in there," Char stated.

"I don't either, but what I want more than anything is to get the hell out of here. The corridors are a maze to nowhere. If we can get past the main lockouts, we may get to a place where we can climb out. I don't know where that is, but I think this access can take us anywhere in the complex."

"They have a complex band-access system, but any knucklehead can crawl through an alternate access? It'll be booby-trapped."

"Of course, it will be."

Char shook her head and removed the same things from her coat as Terry had. She stuffed them into available pockets and dropped to her knees.

"Here's to getting out of here." He toasted her and took a drink of water, less inclined to ration it now that they had found a functioning dining facility.

"You know there's an AI running this place and it's scanning our thoughts."

"I know," Terry admitted. "I can't change any of that, but if it gets me a burger like I just had? I'm good with it. My thoughts are focused on a singular goal. I want to get the fuck out of here. It's not a very good AI if it keeps fucking with us instead of opening the door and letting us walk."

"Maybe it's not because it's studying us."

Terry gave the room the finger, pushed the small, floor-level door open, and gave the finger to what lay beyond.

"It can study that."

He crawled through, with Char right behind him. The

small passage went a short way forward before a lateral conveyor rolled to their right. Straight ahead was another door—the next room. Terry motioned for Char to stay where she was while he pulled himself forward and lifted himself by his toes and fingers to get over the conveyor system and into the cross passage.

He pushed the other door open and found a meeting room set up theater-style with chairs facing a central stage. He didn't see any reason to enter, so he backed up until he was once again straddling the conveyor. It didn't move fast, but he didn't want to get inadvertently sucked away.

"Shall we see where it goes?"

"I have a bad feeling, TH." Char grabbed his ankle.

"We'll take it a little ways and hop off when we see another side corridor. Hang on."

Terry worked his way around the corner, using the small runners on each side of the conveyor to balance himself. "Tracks," he said. "Bots ride on these, and that's how they avoid being pulled away."

He let his body drop the finger width until he hit the independent rollers and started to get pulled. He felt Char bounce around the corner as he accelerated.

They shot past the first side corridor before he could stop them. He let his toes drag along the tracks as he tried to slow down, but the rollers continued to pull him. All of a sudden, the conveyor popped open, revealing a bulk shredder below.

Terry's hands shot out and kept him from falling through. He pressed against the sidewalls with his toes. Spread-eagled, he held his place. Char raced after him, driving her head into his groin. She grabbed his legs and held on.

He gasped in pain and his eyes rolled back in his head, but he hung on. "That hurt a lot."

"I told you it was a bad idea."

"Baseball."

"What?"

Terry began to inch his way backward until he was no longer hanging over the opening. "Baseball. As in a strike on two balls."

"I don't see how you can find that funny." Char grunted as she fought to find her own purchase with fingers and toes.

"A shot in the ghoulies is always funny," Terry mumbled, not sounding amused at all. "Better hurry. Something is coming."

Char pushed herself into a side tunnel and crawled toward the small door, then let her foot dangle to allow Terry to grab it so she could pull them both through. When she felt his hand tighten around her ankle, she pushed the door open, braced herself on the walls, and pulled herself out. She worked her way free and stood. Terry scrambled out and kicked the door shut.

"Some sort of bot. Ugly bastard," he said before looking up to find five faces staring at him. "Hey, fuckers! We meet again."

"We've never met," one of the five who had been in the dining area replied. They stood over their pods and hanging trays within a massive hydroponics lab. One of twelve, if they had heard correctly.

"I'm Terry Henry Walton," Terry said without missing a beat. "And Charumati."

They put both hands on their chests and inclined their heads slightly in the standard greeting of the Erthos.

The five replied in kind.

"We are looking for the elevator to the surface. Or the stairs. Whichever is working."

"I don't believe you can do that," a female Erthos responded. Terry remembered squeezing her doppelganger's neck until she passed out and keeled over dead.

"We seem to be getting that a lot," Char replied in a soothing voice. "Can you show us what you have going on here? This is most impressive."

Terry fell in behind her as she approached the closest worker.

"Sure," the Erthos replied, starting a simplistic monologue on what everything was and their maintenance schedule. She had no working knowledge beyond the tasks they personally performed. Terry frowned with the realization—the degradation of society into set roles. No hope for self-improvement.

But the spark of excitement she relayed when sharing her knowledge gave Terry confidence that no society was beyond hope.

"How do you provide continued nutrition to the plants?" Terry asked, trying to keep the conversation fresh.

"We get the fertilizer from there, a liquid supplement. The water arrives over there, and is distributed through the troughs to here, where it leaves to be recycled," she explained.

"But what's in your fertilizer?" Terry pressed, wanting

her to think deeper. Her compatriots drifted back to their work, delicately pruning, trimming, and picking.

"It's over there. We fill the beakers to the designated line and drop in the right amount for the right plants."

"Yes, I see," Terry replied, placating the young woman even though she didn't answer his question. He knew the reason. She couldn't answer it because she didn't know. "Fertilizer" was the term for a plant additive, nothing more. She didn't know why or how. She only knew that she had to follow the orders.

"Show me how you know which amount goes where," Char interjected.

The Erthos gardener took them to the side of the room, where a number of glass sinks sat in a row. Next to them was a row of beakers upside down on a stand.

"Tomatoes," she said. A yellow light flashed under a beaker, and when she picked it up, a line lit up in yellow. A sink flashed yellow, and in the hydroponics bay, a series of tubs flashed yellow. She filled the beaker to the line from the flashing yellow sink and poured the contents into the correct trough, then rinsed the beaker and returned it to its place on the stand.

"That is the complete process."

So simple, even a caveman could do it, Terry thought.

He thanked her profusely before excusing himself and waved to the others, who paid him no attention, and together, he and Char walked out the door. Once in the corridor, Terry leaned against the wall, resting his head.

"Did we learn anything useful in there?" Terry asked.

"Besides the fact that they have clones, so someone doesn't stay dead for very long."

"I wonder if they know they're clones." Terry hung his head. "It doesn't look like they know too much, and probably not anything to do with them being clones. Rudimentary knowledge. A low baseline."

"At least no one is shooting at us."

"That's because the mean woman whose wristband you're wearing wasn't with them. I expect we'll run into her next and she'll want hers back. Did you see that they were wearing wristbands?"

"I saw. Does that mean the system is going to trigger if it reads what I'm wearing?"

"I'd like to think not because they seem to be haphazard in how they handle intruders."

"I don't want to be an intruder," Char argued.

"You and me both." Terry looked up and down the corridor, chose a direction, and pointed. "The stairway?"

Char nodded, and they headed out.

"I'd feel better with a laser pistol," Char said when they heard a security bot up ahead.

CHAPTER NINE

<u>The War Axe, in orbit around the Efluyez Homeworld, Alganor Sector</u>

"That looks like ass!" Kai declared. Sergeant Capples modeled his dress uniform with integrated ballistic protection. It was bulky and didn't allow for smooth movement, so he marched like a badly made wooden soldier.

"Better ass than grass," Christina shot back.

Kai cocked his head, "The fuck?"

"Dead in the grass. Taking a dirt nap. Root side down, belly side up. Sleep with the fishes..."

"Please, stop," Kai begged, surrendering the field of verbal battle. "It still looks like ass."

"It does," Cory agreed.

"See? Aunt Cory knows it. Mom knows it. You know it. Everyone knows it. Even Grandpa knows it, and he's not even here."

Christina opened her mouth and screamed silently. "Ideas, people! We have three days to get our shit wired, and we're no closer than when we got here. Having the

Black Eagles fly top cover is one thing. Having four mechs out there will reduce our reaction time, but none of that does anything for the troops in the open. Bulky and marching like shit is better than carrying our dead back to the ship."

"Then they won't spring the trap. What do you want, Christina?" Kimber leaned close.

"I want to end the war before it begins by pulling the curtain back to reveal what they want to keep hidden. When the secrets are out in the open, they'll have to come clean. We press them for a treaty and then watch them closely after taking all their money so they don't have enough to start a war."

"Who said Frikanda is the good guy?"

"I expect neither is, but I sure as hell am not going to be anyone's patsy. We're going to march down there, and we're going to pull the trigger before they do."

"Isn't that the million-credit question?" Kimber shook her head. "When do we need to pull the trigger?"

Christina blew a breath past her bottom lip and made her bangs puff into the air. "Back to the drawing board, my boy toy!" she shouted loud enough for all to hear.

Kai rolled his eyes and headed toward the manufacturing area within the *War Axe*.

"That's my son you're talking about," Kimber said, looking for Auburn as she sought moral support. He was nowhere to be seen, but Cory was there.

"My nephew is in good hands," Cory said. "Werewolves and the spouses who love them. Pray that the claws don't come out."

Kimber started to laugh. "The allure of romance with a werewolf."

"It seems to work for our parents." Cory draped an arm over her sister's shoulders. "Can we deny our children the same chance for an enduring love?"

Cory's eyes glistened as she fought back the tears, yet her smile was genuine.

"We boosted our spouses so they would live as long as us," Kimber said, feeling her sister's pain anew. "I'm sorry, Cor. We fight every day so we don't have to fight, and I have a bad feeling about this one."

"I'll be right up front with Chris when we're marching, holding our heads high and waiting for the hammer to fall so we can get to work and do what we do. That's end conflict. Isn't that our tagline? 'A private conflict-resolution enterprise.'"

"You can't be out there. Someone has to come save us. Uncle Ted has been doing a side project for me. He has developed medical stasis chambers that are self-deploying. We only have four constructed at present, and they are under Smedley's control. They will deploy with the company and wait. If someone flatlines, the chamber will scoop them up and secure them. The target is one minute from expiration. After that, we can get them back here and into the Pod-doc for repair and recovery."

Kimber stopped and chewed her lip as her mind walked through recent battles. "We could use a few Pod-doc chambers right here on the hangar deck. Get people fixed up without having to use the elevator or stairs."

"My thoughts exactly. We're going to reconfigure a couple drop cans for that purpose. Four Pod-docs each, controlled from the central core in the med lab. Ted will upgrade that so the system can handle the extra load. It would all be ready by now if it weren't for the attack on Keeg Station. The reconstruction took the supplies and manpower we needed. No matter, it is in the works."

"We still have to march in the parade, though," Kimber countered with a dark scowl. "Christina has something in mind, and I need to know what it is. I can't sacrifice any of our people on the altar of a half-baked plan."

"I think you'll be surprised by what she has in mind," Cory replied before letting her sister go. She walked away without a further word, her head held high and her shoulders back.

Band Rayal Seven, Okkoto

Terry and Char leaned against the wall, trying not to move. Their chests rose slowly with controlled breathing, and their mouths were clamped shut.

The security bot hummed into view and passed them without hesitating. They waited until they could no longer hear it.

"I was ready to give it a good knifing," Terry quipped.

"I guess the wristbands were good or humans are no threat when they're not carrying a dead bot in their arms."

"Or shooting a laser pistol at it." Terry clasped his hands behind his back as he continued to stroll in the direction he thought he would find the stairway. "It didn't try to shoot us either time, did it?"

"I don't think so. Next time, we'll keep walking. I think it will probably pass us by. With these," she held up her arm where the wristband dangled, "we're no longer intruders."

"That's a serious flaw in their security." Terry wasn't amused. "If there's an AI running all of this, wouldn't it adapt?"

"It has *how* many years of no threats to reinforce its processes? Maybe it sees the destruction of the two bots as accidents or system failures. How long can these things operate?"

"Are those six people the only ones here?"

"Seven, if we count Tonie," Terry corrected.

"I thought Tonie was a hologram," Char stated.

"And I'm confused again." Terry shook his head and held out his hand, Char took it, and they walked side by side. With the lights on, they could see everything they needed to see. At the next intersection, Terry looked left. "Cafeteria is down that way, and the elevator. The next left is the way to the quarters area and power station."

Char pointed down the corridor to their right. "We haven't been this way."

Terry pointed forward. "Straight ahead to the stairs, if I remember Tonie's directions."

Char nodded.

"Everything seems to be on one level, so I expect that with twelve hydroponic bays, this place is pretty spread out. That being said, I have no desire to explore it all. I hope to never find out what's in that direction."

"Onward and upward?" Char asked.

"The fault, dear Brutus, is not in our stars, but in ourselves, that we are underlings."

"I shall endeavor not to stab you in the back, dear

Caesar," Char replied.

"A good day this is, that I am not stabbed. I shall persevere through hardships not yet contemplated to not just win this day but to dominate it."

"Uh-huh." Char was never sure what was going to happen when Terry Henry waxed philosophical.

They took the next left and followed the corridor past four doors that remained closed as they walked by. The corridor turned to the right, and four more doors stood between them and where the corridor dead-ended at a massive pile of rubble.

Terry stared at the rubble while he absent-mindedly waved his wrist past the door on his left. Char unintentionally activated the door on the right. Terry and Char jumped into each other, bouncing off to return to where they started.

"Hey there, metal friend!" Terry called in a pleasant voice. A bot identical to the one that fired on them from the lab stood inside with its laser pistol raised.

Char looked at its twin brother in the room she had opened. She raised her hands. "We're playing nice. There's no reason to shoot."

"This corridor is off-limits. You must leave immediately."

"Of course, you rusty pile of gutter trash."

"What are you doing?" Char whispered over her shoulder.

"Dive to your right when I say go," he whispered out the side of his mouth, keeping his eyes on the bot.

"I already don't like it," Char started to say, but Terry was executing his plan.

"I don't think we're going anywhere, Jack, so take your laser pistol and jam it where the sun don't shine! I guess that could be anywhere down here. No matter, prepare your orifice. Here comes one laser pistol."

Terry took one step forward and dove to his right, yelling "Go" as he jumped. Char dodged to her right, the opposite direction of her husband.

Laser fire filled the air and none of it hit the bots, as Char had known it wouldn't. Terry thought it had been worth a shot. He scrambled to his feet and jumped against the wall, slamming his chest into it as he spun around the doorframe to deliver a reverse roundhouse to the bot's metal chest. Terry kicked it hard enough to lift it off the floor and send it crashing back into the room. The robot across the way shot him twice before Terry could fight his way into the room.

Char saw the fire, ducked, and charged. She wrapped up the bot's legs, lifted, and body slammed the device onto the floor. It grabbed her hair and shoved the pistol in her face, but she batted it away and fought with an intense fury that made her eyes glow purple. She started to change; beyond her control, the inner werewolf emerged.

On Terry's side of the corridor, the robot rolled to get to its feet, but Terry delivered a flying stomp to the middle of its back. It pancaked, and he stomped it again before dropping and trying to tear off the metal arm holding the pistol. He twisted and pulled, but it fought back, stronger than his enhanced muscles. They struggled to a stalemate. Terry with his leverage equaled the bot and its strength.

Terry roared with the adrenaline rush and the arm bent. The fingers lost their grip, and the pistol clattered to the floor. Terry lunged, caught the weapon, and rolled to fire into the bot's chest again and again. It slammed into him, and Terry grunted from the pain of the impact and threw the thing off him.

It tumbled to the floor with no light behind its eyes. Terry bolted through the door and across the hallway. A brown werewolf with silver belly fur was running back and forth like a Jack Russell terrier avoiding the laser fire from the bot. Terry delivered a series of shots on target, and the bot started to lose momentum.

Terry pressed the advantage while the bot rerouted systems and prepared to bring itself back to full functionality. From point-blank range, Terry drilled more holes into its chest. Into the area from which he'd ripped the technology in the first bot they killed.

It turned to him and lunged, but the systems failure was complete. Its legs froze before it could complete its attack and the bot fell on its face. Char kicked at the bot and then squatted and peed on the thing's back. Terry grabbed the pistol before it could get befouled and put a few more holes in its head.

The room had an area for repairing robots, and it was already gearing up to fix the one that Terry had damaged. He emptied the laser pistol into the repair equipment and bot-recovery drones, then threw it on the floor near the bot. Char swished by, tail brushing his leg as she passed. Terry backed into the corridor and leaned around the doorframe to shoot the laser pistol. He dodged back when it exploded spectacularly exactly as he had hoped, even though the power pack was spent.

Terry found recovery drones trying to drag the second

bot through a small door at the back like the cleaning bots had done to the bodies in the cafeteria. "Stop!" he ordered. Char bounded through the room, snapping viciously at the small metal creations, and they retreated back into their hole. Terry fired a few more shots into the security bot to make sure it was dead.

"Do you think there are more bots behind the last two doors? Or worse?" Terry asked. The werewolf cocked her head back and forth at him before starting to growl low and dangerous.

"Fine. Let's check it out."

Terry returned to the corridor, looking out before leaving the confines of the security room. Once he was sure the way was clear, he went left, staying close to the wall. Char loped along beside him.

"Watch yourself! I don't want you to get shot." He waved her back, but she wasn't listening. He waved his wristband before the door, and it opened. Terry ducked his head past the door to get a quick look, but the werewolf shot past him. "Dammit!"

He was after her in less than a heartbeat, ready to take on whatever the room threw at him. Inside, Char had one person cornered, the Erthos who had ordered that they be taken. She snapped at the leader's face.

Terry hurried over to grab a handful of fur and Char snapped at him. He fought with her to keep her from biting him, and the purple eyes glowed and sparkled. His shoulders slumped, and his hands dropped to dangle freely. "I'm sorry, Char."

He fixed the cornered Erthos with an angry glare. "I need you to answer some questions."

CHAPTER TEN

<u>The *War Axe*, in orbit around the Efluyez Homeworld, Alganor Sector</u>

"I don't know." Christina frowned and turned the material over. "It seems too light to do the job."

"Let's test it right now. Grab your Jean Dukes Special, dial it to one, and let's see what it does." Kai looked excited. Christina removed her ever-present custom sidearm from its holster.

He wrapped the cloak around himself.

"What are you doing?"

"A live test."

"Bullshit!" Christina holstered her pistol and crossed her arms.

"Boy toy won't get hurt," he taunted.

"Boy toy is going to get plenty hurt, but not by me shooting him. I'll kick your ass upside-down and backwards before I shoot you," she countered.

Kai knew his limits. There were some battles that were worth fighting, but he saw the look on Christina's face and knew for certain this wasn't one of them. Kai hung the cloak on a hook and stepped behind Christina. "Whenever you're ready." He covered his ears.

The colonel pulled her JDS, fired, and holstered it, all in under a second. Together they inspected the cloak. There was a minor scorch mark where the tiny projectile had hit it, but no penetration. The JDS accelerated its ammunition at varying degrees until number eleven on the dial, which was as destructive as a small nuclear weapon. Most people couldn't handle the weapon while firing at that extreme because the kick could break normal bones. It took someone enhanced to attempt it, and only then in limited doses while well-braced.

They tried it on the number two setting, then three. They made it to five before the round penetrated the material.

"Can we call that a successful test?" Kai wanted to get the *War Axe*'s automated production line going as soon as possible.

"Yes. Make them in the same color as the uniforms. We'll call them boat cloaks, and they need to be long enough to cover us right to the ground. We will need helmets, too. I don't want any exposed flesh."

"I'll get these churning. I have everyone's measurements. I'll give you an estimate of production time as soon as I have it, and then we'll start working on the helmets. It's going to be tight."

"We have three days." Christina looked confused.

"We have *only* three days."

. . .

Band Rayal Seven, Okkoto

"There you are!" Bethany Anne called from the doorway.

Terry relaxed. "This means no one is in that room across the way?"

BA nodded in agreement. "It's empty, mostly."

"I don't want to know what that means, but you've seen the stairway. It appears to be blocked by a billion tons of rubble."

"A billion?" BA looked down her nose at Terry's exaggeration. "If you can move enough of it, it looks pretty open."

"You can see inside there?" Terry turned his head but kept his eyes on his prisoner.

BA didn't dignify his question with an answer since she had just told him what she'd seen. Char growled at the Erthos clone.

"I don't know. I've never seen it," she said defensively. "It's always been blocked."

"Then why are you guarding it?"

"We've always guarded it," she replied matter-of-factly.

"Of course, you have." Terry shook his head. "What do we do with you?"

The prisoner looked blankly back at him.

"Why is she still in drag?" BA asked, pointing with her eyes at Char.

"That's a good question. Lover?"

The werewolf started stalking a circle around the room, snapping at TH each time she passed while ignoring Bethany Anne.

"Go away," Terry snarled at the prisoner. "Anywhere but here."

After the door closed behind her, he took a knee and tears started to run down his face. The werewolf studied him before dragging its tongue across his stubble and up his face.

"I love you, Char," Terry mumbled before looking at BA. "Will she be forever in this form?"

Bethany Anne looked at him. "Why am I always saving your ass, Terry Henry Walton?"

A glimmer of hope. A spark of life.

"It's what you do?" Terry ventured.

"As long as it doesn't become a full-time job, I'll let it slide. This time."

BA crouched and focused her attention on the werewolf. "Make that 'this time' once again. Wonderful, I'm being redundant."

Char stopped pacing and blinked quickly. She began to pant, mouth open and tongue flapping with each breath, then howled softly as if sharing her pain. The great brown wolf's body started to change, and with a great sigh, Char was kneeling on the floor, as naked as the day she was born. The silver streak of hair representative of her belly fur in place on the left side of her face

She stood and stretched.

"Thank God!" Terry turned to BA. "Thank you."

"I forgot how to change back," Char said slowly. Rolling her head. "I seem to have misplaced my clothes, but look at that! My wristbands stayed on."

Char shook her hands in the air while Terry selfishly looked at her magnificent body.

"My eyes are up here, mister," she quipped.

"And what beautiful eyes they are! I love that you have a big, bushy tail, but I prefer the human you."

"What a horny bastard," BA trolled before starting to laugh.

"I'll be right back," Terry said and strode past BA, giving her the side eye. She was still laughing.

Char leaned against a small table. The room was austere. "What was she doing in here?" Char asked.

BA took a step to her left. "Who knows what management does when no one's looking? Probably lining up the next worker that she was going to fuck with."

"Thanks, BA. I started to panic. I don't know what happened."

"Old age?" BA quipped. Char smiled at the jest.

"I don't change into a werewolf anymore. It's been so long. I changed through emotion, not intent. I think that messed with me."

The door opened, and Terry came back in. His face was scratched up, and blood trickled from his hair. He handed over Char's clothes and boots. "Your shirt was ripped, but everything else looked like it had been spared. "Hey! You have a crease across your ass."

Char waved a hand impatiently. "What happened to your face?"

"Those little Roomba-wannabes are some mean bastards. I had to dive into the cleaning duct as they were dragging your shit away. The fight didn't last long." He smiled and scrubbed a hand over his face.

"Thanks. I know what you're thinking, and the answer is no. We're not *doing it* down here."

"Where did that come from? And I wasn't thinking that at all, but I am now."

Bethany Anne snorted. "If I had been drinking a Coke, I would have shot it out my nose. Do those Roombas clean up nose Coke?" There was a pause as TH and Char turned in her direction. "Wait. That didn't sound right..."

Char dressed. Before she put on her boots, she showed them to BA, who said, "I love those. I must have a pair. Onyx Station?"

"Keeg!" Char declared. "Thanks to a mutual love of shoes with the station manager, we have a Baxter and Birney with the latest modern and throwback styles."

"Of all the stores that did not survive the ghost ship's attack, Baxter and Birney did, without a scratch. Bizarre, to say the least. No food or hardware, but the shoe store came through. My All Guns Blazing was freaking gutted! I'm still replacing the vats. I have to hide beer on my ship because there is none left on Keeg, but there are women's shoes."

"The universe and fate have delivered the necessities. And please, don't *do it*. If I walked in on that, I'd be scarred for life. I might even have to invent new swear words to help me get through my angst."

Terry's face turned bright red, but Char remained unperturbed.

"Don't worry. You won't."

"Does anyone know what time it is?" Terry asked.

"I feel like I've been up forever."

BA held up her arms and twisted her wrists back and forth. "No watch."

"Forty hours?"

"If we haven't passed it yet, we will soon, and we're no closer to getting out of here than when we started."

"Why is forty hours important?" Bethany Anne asked.

Terry looked at the floor. Char balanced on one foot as she put on a boot. "That was when the shuttle was going to return for us."

BA pursed her lips. "So, is it a one-time bad deal?"

"We can call for it if this thing is still working." Terry produced the comm device the flight attendant had given him. It was scratched and scarred, but the light came on when he pressed the button. "We're going to miss our ride, so we'll have to call for one when we get back to the surface and hope this thing transmits."

"I'm tired and could use a few minutes of sleep," Char said.

Terry nodded in agreement. "What do you say we take Tonie's room and then, you know..."

"We're not *doing it*."

Terry winked at BA.

"Incorrigible. Whatever led me to save you in the first place? You could be a frozen relic, a monument to love, forever trapped in Antarctica," BA mused. She looked over her shoulder. "Gotta run. I'll be back as soon as the next crisis passes." BA wriggled her fingers in a wave as she walked away. "Later, bitches."

The War Axe, in orbit around the Efluyez Homeworld, Alganor Sector

"We're going to look like old Earth vampires," Kimber said. Joseph and Petricia scowled at her.

"For the record, I never wore a cloak. Well, there was that one time. Wait. There were lots of times, but that was in the 1700s! They were all the rage back then."

"You know how fashion has a way of returning. Here we are, Vamp Central. Bad Company rocks the vamp. We are. Clap, clap. *Vampires!*" Christina taunted.

"I thought I knew you," Joseph muttered before working his way to the back of the room.

"Where are you going? You've got to model it for us." Christina pointed to the ballistic cloak Kai was holding.

The mischievous look in her eyes encouraged him more than her order. He was one of the original group, a vampire who had joined Terry Henry Walton in North Chicago many years prior. He lived near them for decades, untrusted by Char and her pack, but Terry had always been honest with him. And once they'd accepted him, they'd risked all for him.

When he and his partner Petricia had been victims of the blood trade, drugged and held for years, their blood siphoned and sold to the rich, Terry and Char had gone to war to find them and bring them home. Terry had personally carried Joseph to safety through gunfire and explosions. He had never asked for thanks, saying it was just what friends did for each other.

Joseph had had friends over the centuries, but only Terry had been willing to die for him.

Maybe he'd never had the right friends. Joseph was at home with the Bad Company, no matter where they were or what they were doing. And Joseph had learned that he, too, would do anything for his friends.

"Why not?" he said, throwing the cloak around himself

dramatically before holding it up to where just his eyes showed in the classic Bela Lugosi rendition of Count Dracula. "I vant to suck your blood!"

The younger warriors looked at him as if he were speaking in tongues. Christina, Kimber, and Auburn clapped. Terry's proclivity toward watching the classics had dragged his whole family along on TH's version of a required classical education.

"No blood-sucking!" Kai declared, even though he knew that with the latest updates to the nanocytes coursing through Joseph's blood, he no longer needed blood of any type for sustenance. He and Petricia were no longer vampires of necessity, but, they would always be as part of their identity.

"I shall not, good sir. It's light, and it swishes gracefully while I walk." Joseph took a few steps to demonstrate. "Good job on the weighting along the lower seam to keep it hanging smoothly."

Joseph marched forward, making a military left turn. The cloak flowed with him without interrupting his stride. "I think we have a winner."

Kai beamed. "Smedley, start the process and churn them out as quickly as you can. Joseph has his in hand. All the rest will need theirs, even our four-legged warriors."

Christina hadn't approved that. She moved close to Kai and whispered into his ear, "Why do they need them?"

"If shit goes down, they'll run into the middle of it. Look who you're keeping out of the mix. Those are three of our best, and they are the most likely to survive an extreme whatever-it-may-be."

"I'll hold them in reserve, but it never hurts to have

some extra protection." Christina kissed Kai on the cheek. "How long until they're ready?"

"Twenty hours," Smedley replied.

"Sounds good. What do you have for helmet designs?" Christina pressed.

"My God, woman!" Kai blurted. "All your good ideas create more work for me."

"And you are a better man for it." She prepared to leave before turning serious. "We're jumping into the mouth of the volcano. If any of this stuff gets fucked up, we're going to get our own people killed. I don't want that."

"No one wants that. Let's take a look. Joseph? Maybe there are some helmet designs from the 1700s that we could use."

"Surely you jest. Get one of these tech-savvy folks. I've done my good deed for the day, and I'm off to re-watch a couple old films. I don't think I have my accent exactly correct."

"Christina?" Kai said softly as he followed her toward the door. She watched the others leave and her shoulders dropped.

"Fine. I'll keep you company, and I have some ideas."

CHAPTER ELEVEN

<u>Band Rayal Seven, Okkoto</u>

Terry and Char pulled a few of the smaller rocks from the fall. Terry started to move bigger rocks, trying to clear out the top of the fall to see what was beyond.

"Look out below!" he called from his perch as he grunted with the effort to move some of the bigger boulders. Char jumped out of the way to let one roll past her, then scrambled up the fall to join him.

"Not tired anymore?" she asked.

He looked at her through bloodshot eyes. "Exhausted, but if our way out is two rocks away? I'd kick myself for spending one extra minute in this nuthouse."

"If we get through and then have to fight?" Char continued to move smaller stones to clear handholds on the next boulder, then together they shoved the monster out of the way. It shook the pile as it tumbled to the floor.

"We've only been up for maybe a couple days. We can manage a while longer."

"In our younger days," Char clarified. "Today, not so

much. We need to conserve our energy."

As if trying to prove her wrong, Terry leveraged a massive boulder by himself, pushing it aside. Once done, he proved her right. "Fuck, that hurt," he grumbled. He laid on his stomach and shined his flashlight into the gaps. "More rocks."

"Let's call it a day. We can hit it again tomorrow." Char helped TH to his feet. "We can stop by the dining area and get a snack and something to drink before getting some rest."

"Chow and sleep! A Marine's two favorite words."

Char nodded knowingly. They walked lightly and listened carefully as they passed their turnoff to get to the rooms and continued to the next intersection, where they intended to take a right, go three doors down on the left, and dine in peace.

But the female Erthos leader had a different idea.

"There they are!" she declared and pointed with her arm completely outstretched.

"We have a laser pistol now," Char whispered.

"These dipshits are so fragile that one punch kills them. I don't want to shoot them. We need the pistol if we run across more bots."

"Wait," Char stated and walked forward with her hands up. Terry tried to stuff the laser pistol in his pockets, but they were already too jammed with other stuff. He settled for holding it in one hand while he kept the other on his Ka-bar. "We don't want to be here any more than you want us here. Can you please help us to get out? We fell down an elevator shaft over there, and all I want is to get home to my kids!"

Char turned on the waterworks, weeping as she stopped and let her head hang, exposing Terry's face behind her. He tried to look equally solemn and nodded for effect. He wasn't sure they bought it, but it did confuse the three, the mean leader and two newcomers, who were standing in the corridor.

"We ask only for your help. Please?" Char walked forward with her arms out.

"Why do you have a wristband?" the mean leader demanded.

"So we can eat something to keep up our strength while we search for a way out." Char hadn't hesitated at all before delivering her reply. What monster would deny food to refugees?

They had apparently just met her.

She sneered mightily, recovering her wits and ordering the other two to action. "Seize them!"

In a flash of speed almost too quick for the eye to follow, Char delivered a finger-punch to the Erthos leader's throat. She gasped and clutched at her neck, staggered, and dropped to her knees. Her face turned purple before she fell over.

The other two still hadn't moved.

"Tell me the way out of here." Char grabbed the Erthos by their shirts and pulled them to her. "I'm done fucking around."

"I-I don't know a way out," one stammered.

"We work in hydroponics," the other added as if that told the whole story.

"Then you should get back to work. Don't worry about her. I suspect she'll be back before you know it," Terry offered and winked at the two before working his way past them to pick up the dead leader and carry her surfboard-style to the dining room.

Char followed, checking over her shoulder as the two continued to stand in the intersection. Terry activated the door and went in, dumping the body unceremoniously on the table.

"Two double burgers, one order of curly fries, and a massive chocolate shake."

Char looked at him. "You're going to eat that right before going to sleep?"

"Yes, I am, and I also want to see that it will make exactly what I am expecting. Testing a hypothesis."

The device on the wall delivered exactly what Terry had envisioned. He took his tray, sat down at the table closest to the door, not far from the dead Erthos, and started stuffing his face.

"Why did you bring her along?"

"Another hypothesis. I suspect when the little cleaner bots pick something up, they report it, and a new one gets made. If they don't recover her, then maybe they won't make another one. Three times we've encountered her, and all three times she was a total bitch. I don't want there to be a fourth."

Another massive bite and slow chewing to savor his meal.

Char ordered a chicken Caesar salad and a large sweetened ice tea. When they arrived, she sniffed the salad. She shrugged her satisfaction and sat down on the far side of TH, keeping him between her and the body. She wasn't squeamish, but he'd put the deader on the table.

She kept glancing at it.

"I can't put it on the floor. Those sneaky little bastards will drag it away." Terry pointed to the space that they'd crawled through earlier. Even as close as they were, they couldn't see the door's outline because of how well it blended into the wall. They hadn't missed something obvious, but it reinforced Terry's initial approach of treating the place like Wolfenstein.

He finished eating quickly but drew the chocolate shake slowly through the wide straw.

"We need these at the All Guns. I think they'd be a big hit."

"You know they would, but how would you make one? We can't quite get the usual ingredients."

"We overcame all obstacles with the now-famous Moonstokle Pie, outer space's legal version of the bacon and pineapple. We can overcome the chocolate shake hurdles."

"Do you think they're going to bother us again?" Char asked after her last bite.

"They let us eat in peace." He shook his head. "I don't think anyone is in charge. They've been down here too long with a computer generating a minimum standard product. These people are halfwits. They have zero drive because they've never learned to ask questions or how to think."

"The one giving us the tour of hydroponics had a spark."

"I think that is something that can never be completely tamped down, but it would take a lot of nurturing to show her what to do with that. Down here? They probably kill the inquisitive and make another. Which makes me wonder, where did they get the burger for these things?" Terry looked skeptically at his empty plate, smirking. "It was so good."

"Lab-grown meat. It was a thing on Earth before the World's Worst Day Ever. It's not farfetched to believe that they mastered it here, making it to exacting specifications to get the desired flavor and doing it instantly. Or you just ate the previous version of her." Char pointed with her chin at the corpse.

"If it *was* her, she made a great burger."

"Are you bringing her to the room?"

Terry smiled innocently but didn't answer, choosing to take a drink from his shake instead. Char took her tray back to the food processing device and put it inside, something they had not done on their previous visit. A few moments later, it was gone.

"Time to go, lover," Char told her husband.

Terry delivered his tray as Char had done but hung onto the shake. He vacuum-sucked the remainder and then ordered another one. When it arrived, he put the empty inside and walked away.

He handed Char the laser pistol. With the body clutched surfboard-style under one arm and the shake in the other, he was out of hands.

Char went first, checking the corridor for surprises before heading out. Terry followed. She walked quickly, hesitating at the corners to peek around them before continuing. The corridors were empty and quiet as they hurried to the room they had identified as Tonie's.

Terry leaned toward the door so his wristband could

activate it. When it slid open, they expected to see Tonie inside, but the room was empty, exactly as they had left it many hours before.

They weren't sure how long it had been, and that in and of itself was disconcerting.

"It's like being tortured, where they mess with your sleep and meals and time," Terry suggested.

Char took the bed, and after stuffing the corpse in the shower, Terry took the recliner. Once seated and relaxed, with the wristband on, he found himself surrounded by holographic screens. He tapped a couple and found they were interactive.

"So they *do* have technology for the unwashed masses."

"They must not use it, or it's so dumbed-down that they don't get anything from it." Char tried to see from the bed, but her eyes drooped. Terry blinked the screens into focus but decided to stop fighting it.

He climbed from the recliner and jammed his Ka-bar into the track to keep the door from retracting into the wall should anyone try to enter, then checked the door. It refused to open.

"Looking good." Terry smiled at his work and turned to Char for her approval, but she was already asleep. He sat down on the recliner and leaned back. He didn't remember falling asleep, but he didn't think he'd been out for long when the pounding started. Someone wanted into their room.

Efluyez Homeworld, Alganor Sector

Christina looked at three different helmet designs,

unhappy with all of them. Too weak, but great vision. Poor vision, but strong. Too bulky. "There has to be something else," she moaned.

"No one was any help." Kai leaned back from the design screen and shook his head. He rubbed his eyes with his knuckles. "I need a break."

"Did you ask Ted?"

"I said that I need a break, not more abuse."

"Come on, my big, tough man. Let's go see the scary werewolf."

Kai tossed his head like a little kid not wanting to go to school, and Christina started to laugh. Her boyfriend was only seventy-five years old. She always hid her age, but she was over one-fifty. The ways of the nanocyte-enhanced were not the same. Age differences didn't matter. Compatibility was more important because once committed, those with long lives were in it forever.

And forever is a very long time indeed.

When Kai stood, Christina embraced him, their faces nearly touching as their eyes met. "Why is this problem biting you?" she asked.

"I have to get it right, given all your talk of an ambush that you are gleefully going into. You are trusting me to fabricate something that looks showy but will protect you like the universe's greatest chastity belt."

"I think we're past the chastity-belt stage," she quipped.

He poked her in the stomach, and she bit his ear. His eyes sparkled as he pulled away. He reached for her again, but she stonewalled him with an outstretched hand.

"Ted first."

"You have made getting belittled by Ted a delight."

"Who's saying he's going to belittle you?"

Kai looked at her from under a furrowed brow. "He's Uncle Ted. It's what he does."

"And he doesn't mean anything by it. He dedicates a zillionth of his brainpower to social interactions, that's all. Be nice, because he will remember forever if you aren't. We should take him food. I guarantee he hasn't eaten."

"What does he like?"

"How long have you been with him?" Christina asked.

"Not as long as you!" Kai gestured toward the door. "We'll figure it out."

Neither had any idea what Ted liked to eat, so they called in the expert. *Smedley, contact Felicity and ask her what Ted likes to eat, please.*

I have insight into your request. Felicity has ordered me to report on his meal schedule. How long it's been since he last ate dictates what meal I am to order for him. It has been only eight hours, so it would be a peanut butter and jelly sandwich with what used to be known as a "Red Bull."

We'd like to take those to him. Where are they, and where is he? Christina requested.

You can get his meal from Jenelope on the mess deck, and he is in the Combat Information Center.

Roger, Smedley. You've been a great help, Kai replied

"Did you ask Smedley for help with the helmets?" Christina wondered.

"He was no help at all."

They hurried to the mess deck, where it was between formal meal times, although it was always open. Jenelope was the master chef, and Xianna, a warrior's spouse, was helping as part of riding on the *War Axe* with her husband.

She was a lithe, green female from Torregidor. They'd had to intervene to keep her from walking naked around the ship. Social norms on her home planet were far different from what the human leadership of the Bad Company could tolerate.

Before they could speak, Jenelope pointed at the counter with her carving knife.

"Is that a can?" Kai asked as he studied the silver and blue can with the red lettering.

"It's how he likes it," Jenelope replied without looking up. She didn't expound because she didn't need to. Her short statement told them everything they needed to know.

"You are the best!" Kai said as he walked around the counter to give the head chef a hug.

"I have a knife," she taunted him, waving it menacingly.

"You shall cut me to find my undying love pouring out."

"That's one way to put it." She dodged him gracefully before wrapping him in a bear hug of her own. Xianna ran over and embraced them both before planting a kiss on Kai's cheek. He flushed as he sought Christina's eyes.

She watched him intently.

"That's enough, my most favorite people on the whole ship. Well, second most. Maybe even third, but it's because I am me."

"Go on, you derelict!" Jenelope waved her knife at him. "And back to work with you, too!" She pointed at Xianna, who laughed and waved, dancing her way back to where she was preparing fresh greens for dinner.

As they left, Christina studied him. He stopped in the corridor. "You're not jealous, are you?"

"Should I be?"

"That's a setup question." He stood back and posed, turning left and then right. "Does this make me look fat?"

"Now you understand."

"I don't understand a thing," Kai countered, confused to the point of not being able to reply further.

Christina started walking. "Helmets. To keep our heads from getting blown apart."

"A sobering thought." He looked at the floor as they walked. "I don't want you to walk into an ambush. I like you too much for that."

"Like?" Christina turned back to him.

"I don't know what love is," he admitted. "I know that I'd be lost without you. I may flirt too much, but my heart is in one place. And I have to admit that the flirting has lost its allure, especially seeing you watching. I feel like I've betrayed you, but our relationship is based on fun. Or it used to be. Now, it's more a part of my soul. I only wanted to have fun with you, but I won't be able to tolerate losing you. Don't die!"

Kai headed for the stairs to descend to the deck where the CIC was located.

"I have no intention of dying. That's why I want a helmet to protect my head and a cloak to keep my body from getting ripped apart. For the record, I've gotten used to your company, too."

He stopped mid-step and started to kneel. She grabbed him and held him upright.

"And if you ever propose to me, it better not be on this fucking ship!"

"You are a continuing challenge to my meager

existence."

"And I'm not even trying." She smiled at him. "Yet. And we better have our clothes on, too."

"So many conditions. Is there anything left? I'm fresh out of ideas."

"You sound like Terry Henry Walton." Christina held his stare.

Kai gave her his most winning smile. "He is the coolest and hardest man I know. I'll take that as a compliment."

"Why am I in love with the least romantic man in the universe?"

"But I am so loveable..."

She rolled her eyes, shook her head, and continued the short walk to CIC, where they expected to find Ted. Kai smiled at the slight skip to her step.

The CIC was darkened to improve screen clarity. They found Ted in the middle of a holosphere he had created from the center's holoscreens. The sphere gave him more interactive screen space than the cylinder and a shorter response time for manipulation and orchestration.

"Ted," Christina said. She cleared her throat and said his name louder.

Kai reached through the images, and Ted stabbed his fingers into the intruding arm.

"I'm in the middle of something. Go away!" Ted shouted.

"We need your help to design a new combat helmet that we can wear in the parade. We need the design in the next twenty minutes or we're all going to die." Christina tried to look innocent despite her exaggeration. Kai nodded vigorously.

"Heads exploding everywhere. Big death." Kai tried to be supportive.

"Less help," Christina whispered harshly.

"Fine," Ted said, but never stopped tapping and working the three-dimensional projections surrounding him. Kai and Christina waited, shifting uncomfortably as time dragged on.

"Uncle Ted?" Kai ventured.

"You're still here? I sent it to Smedley. Manufacture has begun. Now, go away. I'm busy."

"That's cool. Thank you, Uncle Ted," Kai said. Once out in the corridor, they realized that they still had Ted's lunch. Kai handed the Red Bull to Christina and she returned to the CIC.

"Almost forgot. Here's your lunch. Felicity says you're supposed to eat. Peanut butter and jelly with a Red Bull."

Ted didn't answer, but a finger pointed to his feet while he continued his intricate weaving and holographic-screen tapping. Christina put the bag and can on the floor at his feet and slowly backed out.

Kai was waiting. "Now that that's over, it looks like we have some time to kill."

"Incorrigible." She slapped his hand away as he reached for her, then turned and bolted, almost running over Dokken. "Sorry, buddy, busy."

She ran a hand down his back before continuing on her way.

"Sorry, buddy," Kai called as he raced after Christina.

Humans, the dog lamented. *So shallow. That reminds me. I'm hungry. Let's see what's for dinner.*

CHAPTER TWELVE

<u>Band Rayal Seven, Okkoto</u>

"Fuck off!" Terry bellowed as he tried to focus. He stood up, slightly wavering. "Nope, not enough sleep."

The pounding stopped with his yell but started up after a few moments.

Char sat up in bed. "Your vacations suck."

"Now you know why I work all the time," Terry agreed.

Char raised her laser pistol. Terry took a few deep breaths and put on his war face, ready to battle with whatever waited beyond the door. He counted down on his fingers and yanked the knife from its place holding the door closed, and it instantly slid to the side. Outside stood Tonie, red-faced and out of breath.

"This is my room," he said, outrage clear on his face.

"I thought you meant for us to use it when you gave me your wristband," Terry said, quickly reaching out to find a solid being. Terry's hand recoiled of its own volition, and he forced himself to reach out and poke the Erthos.

"Ouch!" Tonie looked put out. "What's wrong with you?

Don't you have someplace else to be?"

"You don't sound like the others," Char said, not stating what she was thinking. He sounded intelligent and apparently had an independent mind.

"I am so sorry. I misunderstood. My wife knew better, but I talked her into it. Please accept my apologies." Terry checked his pockets. He was disappointed that he wouldn't get a shower. Char checked her gear as well and followed Terry into the corridor. "Oh, and there's a dead body in your shower."

Tonie hurried in and the door closed. They waited. When the door opened, Tonie's face was pale. "W-why did you kill Lucinda?"

"Lucinda tried to have us taken into custody, and we simply cannot have that," Terry explained. "We're trying to leave, and it looks like we'll get no help in finding our way out of this place."

"I have to report this."

"Do what you have to do," Terry mumbled, too tired to argue. "But know this: I will kill every single person in this complex if I have to. We came down an elevator shaft, and it pains me to believe there's no way for that elevator to return to the surface. Someone will help us or everyone will perish. That's not a threat, but this place has been hostile to us since we arrived. That female in there? Killed her twice.

"There were some nice folks in one of the hydroponics labs, and you were exceedingly kind. Maybe it's time for everyone to simply stay out of our way. We'll take care of it. Just stop shooting at us, and stop trying to fight us."

"I see," Tonie said. "Take the body, and I won't report

you."

"Sure," Terry said. He didn't want to, but it was the best option at the moment. He returned tc the hallway with Lucinda on his hip. She'd started to stiffen.

The door closed, leaving the two humans and their dead Erthos.

"Can we ditch the stiff?" Char asked. Terry nodded toward the power room at the end of the corridor and strolled that way. The door opened for him, and he tossed the body inside. He rubbed his hands on his pants and returned to Char.

"I bet we'll run into Lucinda Three before this day is out."

"Probably, but we're not going to kill everyone down here."

"No, although I have a tendency toward extreme violence when I'm tired and people shoot at me."

"We'll just have to shoot them right back." Char started walking, her steps mechanical, barely with a purpose.

"Let's go move some more rocks," Terry suggested.

"What if the security bots have been replaced? I'm not in any shape to fight them."

"Nor I." Terry had to make a concerted effort not to drag his feet. "Why am I so tired? I must be out of shape."

"You're not out of shape, you've been up for too long. Just like me. Don't make me say it again. Stop beating a dead horse, and let's find a place to get some sleep. Even this floor looks comfortable."

Terry grumbled his consent and they slow-walked back the way they'd come, taking every right until they arrived at the first room they'd entered. The lab. When the door opened, Terry and Char dodged out of the way, expecting another robot, but this time, the room was empty.

The door shut behind them and Terry jammed his Kabar into the slot, wedging the mechanism to give them some privacy. He toed the wall as he shuffled along it until he found the secret cleaning access door, dumped a heavy metal table on its side, and slid it against the opening.

"Let them have peace. The peace of heaven is theirs that lift their swords, in such a just and charitable war," Terry quoted Shakespeare.

"If they demand a war, let it start here!" Char added. "After a decent rest, of course."

Her eyes closed, and she was out. Terry stroked the silver streak in her hair. "I will move heaven and Earth so you may walk out of here." He laid on the floor next to the table where Charumati slept and closed his eyes, but sleep remained elusive. What if they were trapped forever beneath five hundred feet of Okkoto's bedrock?

In orbit above the Efluyez Homeworld, Alganor Sector

"I don't like your plan." Captain Micky San Marino shook his head. "Not in the least. We have to return to orbit after we've dropped you into the cauldron?"

"You make it sound like you're serving us up to savages," Christina replied. "I'll personally kick their leadership in the balls if one-tenth of what I'm expecting happens. How many of their own are they willing to sacrifice?"

"All of them? Remember what Nero did to Rome?" Kai interjected.

"How old do you think I am?" Christina shot back before she realized he wasn't speaking about anything more than a knowledge of history. "Yes, he burned Rome so it could be rebuilt as he wanted, bypassing the Senate."

"All of them. Look for the Magnate. If he's there, you might be safe, unless it's one of his scheming inner circle. Wouldn't be the first time an insider killed the boss to take over," Micky said, nodding slowly after thinking it through

"I'll ask for a list of dignitaries who will be attending, and more importantly, who won't be attending. We'll run that through Smedley's outstanding facial recognition subroutines to come up with a list of the missing. Maybe we can forestall the damage, find our perp, and have a great parade that doesn't end in fireworks." Christina held her hands up as if that was it. End of discussion.

"Smedley, get me the Magnate."

"He is unavailable, it appears, but the Executive Secretary is most eager for a conversation."

"I bet he is. Put that fucking putz on the line."

"He already is," Smedley said softly.

She shook her head slowly. "Mister Executive Secretary. I require a list of everyone who will be in attendance at the parade."

"We don't have such a list."

"Then just the dignitaries will do. We need to know who we're going to salute when the time comes. It'll be a magnificent tribute!" she declared with a flourish.

"The only one you need to salute is the Magnate. Now, if I can get in a word, it won't do that you met with the Frikandans. That won't do at all. We're considering canceling our contract with you."

"Fucking do it!" she blurted before sucking her lips in and casting a guilty look at Micky. He shrugged his indifference to her approach but supported her intent.

"You seem to be uncaring about half a million credits. Most organizations would bend over backwards for such a sum to be paid for only four hours' work."

"Listen here, you fucking toad. We don't need your money, but didn't like a hole in our schedule. We thought we could help you and a little parade never hurt anyone, but I've about had it with you. Don't jack us around, you little fuckwad. Let me talk with the Magnate directly."

"That is not going to happen," the toad replied. "I cannot put a common soldier in front of the greatest one who has ever lived."

"When this is over, I'm going to find you, and you will regret the day you were born. And if the Magnate does not show up for the parade, you will be the first one I hunt down for answers."

"I can't imagine what answers anyone would owe bottom-dwelling sea creatures such as the Bad Company."

Christina fumed. She gritted her teeth and growled, and Kai poked her in the shoulder. His toothy grin met her fury.

"He's baiting you," he whispered. She straightened and threw her head back.

"I appreciate you sending us the list. We'll head to the surface when we have it in hand. It would be a pity to leave before we march, but if we don't have the complete list of at least the dignitaries, we will not be able to march in your parade. We've been practicing twenty-nine hours a day to get it right. Pity. This is the *War Axe*, signing off. Toodles!"

"Nice comeback," Kai told her.

Micky grimaced. "I better make sure the weapons systems are operating at peak performance. That conversation did not instill confidence."

"Me either, Skipper," Christina admitted. "We better check on those helmets." She took Kai's hand, and they left the bridge.

The captain looked at his small bridge crew. Clifton and Ruzfell went about their duties while waiting for the captain to issue an order. "Immediate response drills for weapons. Notify Engineering that we'll be conducting drills until we get the word to return to the planet."

"When will that be, sir?" Ruzfell asked.

"Not for a while, I suspect."

"Prepare for Intra-atmospheric Weapons Engagement Drill Alpha," Micky ordered and leaned back to watch the crew in action.

Band Rayal Seven, Okkoto

Terry rolled over and bumped his head against the table leg, which startled him awake. He smacked his dry lips before pulling a pouch of water from his pocket. He took a long drink, downing half of it before re-sealing it. He was hungry even though he remembered that he had eaten right before he'd laid down. *Could have been four hours or fourteen.*

He stood and stretched, assuming a few yoga positions to welcome the new day. While Char continued to sleep, he did a quick inventory of what he carried. A little food in the way of the protein bars that came in the jacket, the multi-tool, the flashlight, and a single water pouch. His Ka-bar was wedged in the door. Combined, it wasn't much, but he also had his hands, which were deadly weapons or tools, whatever he needed them to be. He flexed his digits, knowing they would get a workout during the upcoming day.

"Are you ready to roll some stone?" he asked them. The fingers, as they were wont to do, did not respond.

He checked the table blocking the cleaning bot access, which was undisturbed. He wouldn't pull his Ka-bar out until Char was awake, so he sat on the floor and ran through everything they knew about the place.

Elevator shaft. No cable, traction driven. A door had slammed shut above them after they'd descended. Even if they climbed upward, they'd be stymied by that. They needed the elevator to work so it could ascend, opening the door as part of its normal operation.

The outpost. A survival site in case of an attack on the moon's surface. Cut off. Not Kurtherians, but powered by the Etheric. Race looks human and is up on human tastes, which they couldn't possibly be. A chocolate milkshake? Locked down here for how many millennia?

Clones. Recycled beings. No self-motivation. Little more than drones, except Tonie. He seemed to think for himself, and he was solid. Bethany Anne's hand had gone right through him. Maybe she was the ghost.

But not a ghost. Existing across the Etheric through a door that was opened when they broke the seal? How could she help them if she was only there in spirit? "Show us the way, my Queen," Terry whispered almost as a prayer.

CHAPTER THIRTEEN

"How early do you hard-rubbing nut-lovers get up?" Bethany Anne asked, kneeling next to TH.

"What time is it?"

"I still don't know." BA smirked. "What time do you think it is?"

"This is why I would never, ever, no matter how long I live, go to a therapist. I just want to know the time. I feel rested, so I'm going to go with morning. That works for me, whether it is or isn't."

BA stood. "Was that so hard?"

"As a hard-rubbing nut-lover can get," Terry replied. Char stirred and propped herself up on one elbow.

"Good morning," Char offered.

"I rest my case." Terry stood up. "I could use a cup of coffee. I hope the chow hall is open."

"Dining facility," Char corrected.

"We agree. It needs to be open. Did you see a bathroom anywhere in your travels? I'd hate to impose on Tonie since that's the only one I saw."

BA shook her head. She appeared to lean against the wall.

"Are you real?" Terry asked.

"What kind of clusterfucked brain-boiled question is that?"

Terry started to reach toward her.

BA's lips pressed tightly together. "I will reach down your throat and pull your nutsack out through your mouth," she warned.

Terry considered the risk versus the reward before deciding to put his hand down. "Sounds like you. I have a theory—"

Char coughed. "Is it a long or short one? I could use a bathroom."

"Me, too. I'll talk as we walk." Terry looked at BA. "Is the passage clear?"

She held her hands up and shrugged.

"Fine." Terry made sure Char was ready, laser pistol in hand before he yanked his Ka-bar out. The door immediately popped open, revealing the well-lit and empty corridor beyond. Terry waved his wristband at each of the three doorways on both sides of the hallway. When he reached the intersection, he went straight toward the dead end to check the remaining six doors.

The first one opened—a storeroom that was mostly filled. Once sure there was no one inside, he entered and checked the shelves and stacks. "I don't read Kurtherian."

"But you do," Char remarked. "Your chip translates it. If you can't read it, then it's not Kurtherian or any other language that the chip knows."

"We can understand them. I think they are speaking present-day English."

"That's what I hear too, without the usual delay between their mouths moving and what my brain hears."

"BA?" Terry asked.

"I am at a complete loss, TH."

"It's like a really sucky game of Clue," Terry said before picking up a couple small pieces from a bin. "I don't know what any of this stuff is."

Char joined him while BA waited in the corridor. "Why is this stuff here? Wouldn't spare parts be close to their point of use?"

"In a perfect world. We don't know what's behind the other doors in this corridor."

"And this isn't getting us closer to a bathroom."

"A shower would be nice," Terry admitted.

"Ooh," BA crooned from the corridor, standing with her arms across her chest.

"You stuffed me into a Pod-doc, so you've already seen all there is. And I have to thank you again for saving my life. Antarctica sucked more than this game of Clue that we appear to be losing."

"You've been a good member of my team. Akio says hi, by the way."

"I love that guy!" Terry blurted. Char chuckled before heading to the next door. She waved her angry-female-Erthos wristband at it and it opened to a sprawling room that spread into the distance.

"Bingo." Terry and BA looked in.

"Lots of stuff going on in there." From one movement

to another, they followed as they tried to figure out what the active systems were being used for.

"Manufacturing using print-on-demand technology for everything from spare parts to people?" BA offered.

Terry and Char nodded. "The people part is disconcerting, but they had to be built somewhere."

The three entered the complex. "It looked so innocent as a non-descript door among other non-descript doors in a plain corridor," Char said.

"Would you look at who's here to greet us? It's the mean woman called Lucinda!" Terry exclaimed.

"I got this," BA said as she sauntered toward her. Char looked enviously at her boots.

"We'll find where she got them, and we'll get you a better pair," Terry whispered. Char responded by taking his hand as they waited for the Queen to engage.

"We're looking for a bathroom," Bethany Anne said evenly.

"Out the entrance. First door on your left."

"Thank you. You've been very kind." BA turned to walk away but stopped and looked back over her shoulder. "And can you tell us the way to the surface of this moon?"

Terry and Char backed toward the entrance. When the door opened, Char headed out and sighed when the next door opened and it was a bathroom. Terry stood where he could see both the corridor and BA.

"No, I can't tell you that."

"Can't or won't? There is a difference." Bethany Anne began exploring Lucinda's mind, but hers was different. She was human, but not. Her thoughts were controlled, held behind barriers that seemed not of her making, as if a third party could unlock what it needed upon command. BA's mind knocked on the doors within the woman's thoughts, but she couldn't open them. "'Can't' it is."

Char returned and stood at the entrance as Terry took his turn.

BA left the Erthos leader and started strolling but didn't get very far.

Lucinda stood with back arched and arm stretched to full length as she pointed at Bethany Anne. "Seize her!"

There were no other people or hardware that they could see.

"Good luck with that, dumbass." BA continued her stroll, her hands clasped behind her back as she looked at various machines.

Char waited. She leaned into the corridor and yelled, "Put the book away, TH!" She shook her head and mumbled. "Men."

Laser beams stabbed across the space and into Bethany Anne. She looked down as they passed harmlessly through her body. She pursed her lips and shook a finger at the Erthos female.

Char braced herself against the door, ready to go in or out as the situation dictated. Terry finally returned, still fastening his pants.

"All good!" he declared before asking, "What did I miss?"

"They fired lasers from somewhere, but they went through BA's body. She's ignoring them. I think she's walking the Etheric."

"Is that common?" More lasers fired, which scorched and burned the equipment and wall behind Bethany Anne.

"I have heard it was possible but didn't know anyone who could actually do it."

"What is it?" Terry asked, grimacing at his ignorance of the Etheric.

"Take their body into the Etheric and go anywhere they want. I think it's a higher level of evolution. Maybe Michael can do it, too."

Two robots of the type Terry and Char encountered when they first entered the outpost appeared, but before they could get close, explosions sparked from their chests and they tumbled helplessly to the floor. With a final spasm, each bot settled as so much scrap.

"That was interesting." Terry craned his head back and forth to see if anything else was coming.

"She killed their Etheric power sources."

"If we only had some popcorn, we could watch this appropriately." Terry started to walk in, but Char stopped him.

"We are not invulnerable like she is. As you'll remember, lasers hurt."

"Only too well, my lover," Terry agreed. When he looked up, BA was nowhere to be seen and the Erthos leader was pointing at them.

"Seize them!"

"Shoot her!" Terry replied in the same tone and volume.

Char raised her laser pistol but didn't fire. "Maybe we shouldn't kill her again."

She put the pistol into her pocket.

"She'll be back when we don't want her to be. Bring her with us?" Terry asked.

"I'm not sure how that will work, but we can try it. This place is more like *Groundhog Day* than Clue, I think."

"We're spinning our wheels, constantly ending up where we started." Terry pointed toward the first room where he'd been drilled by the robot's laser. That was where they'd just spent the night.

"Except we keep finding little tidbits, crumbs that could be leading us somewhere."

"Everywhere but out of this fucking shithole." Terry stormed up to Lucinda and grabbed her by the arm.

"Seize them!" she shouted in his face.

"Why don't you seize me yourself, you miserable woman?"

"It's not one of my duties," she countered, trusting the pragmatism of her argument.

"You're coming with us, and you know what? That *is* in my job description, for right now, anyway. You ever hear of cross-training?"

"No. It is not one of my duties." She took a deep breath as she prepared to yell. Terry poked her in the abdomen, driving upward with his finger to force the air from her lungs. The air exploded from her, and she started to cough.

"Do not yell in my face. Or my ear, or anywhere near me. If you yell, you get poked." Terry kept hold of her arm and forced her to walk with him as he toured the space, looking for something he might be able to use in his search for an exit.

Like something to help them move those rocks.

Char joined them. "Hi, Lucinda," she greeted the woman as if they were meeting for the first time.

The Erthos kept her mouth shut, torn between being

afraid of Terry Henry Walton and defiant in giving no information to the intruders.

As they walked, they discovered that few of the machines were running. "That's why it's so quiet," Terry noted.

"Is this the main manufacturing hub for the outpost?" Char looked at Lucinda for an answer. She kept her mouth shut.

"Life will be so much better if you answer our questions. We're not asking you to betray your people or your position. Is there anything in your job description that says you can't answer questions? What about yelling 'seize them?' I can't believe you have a duty that directs you to yell that."

Lucinda looked confused.

They waited.

"It doesn't say exactly that."

"Then what *does* it say, exactly?" Char asked, keeping her voice even and free of emotion.

"To protect the sanctity of our home..." Her words drifted into obscurity as she couldn't end her thoughts.

Terry stopped and pointed at the laser scorch marks on one of the machines, following them across to where they left a pencil-thin line along the wall. "Who caused that damage?"

"The security crew."

"On your orders, which means you caused the damage. We haven't harmed anything. What are you doing by damaging your home?" Terry urged her to find an answer that would help them escape the outpost. He didn't mention the robots they had killed in self-defense.

"Are you a dog?" Lucinda suddenly asked.

Terry pointed to himself and shook his head. Char knew who the Erthos leader was talking about.

"I believe you see who you're talking to. Do I look like a dog?"

"No," Lucinda conceded.

"What makes you ask that? Do you remember what happens to previous versions of yourself? Our impression was that you do not." Char analyzed the Erthos clone clinically, seeking scientific information. She treated her like an experimental subject and not a potential friend.

They had already killed her more than once so they couldn't begrudge her animosity.

"I don't know what you are talking about. Claymore told me that I should ask."

Terry and Char's ears both perked up. "Who is Claymore?" Char inquired as Terry studied their captive.

"Claymore directs all for the Erthos."

Char chewed on the information. Terry jumped in. "Can we speak to this Claymore?"

"You may not. He won't allow it."

"How do you speak with him?" Terry asked.

"I just know what he says. It's like he speaks to me in a dream."

"How does he know what a chocolate milkshake is?"

"I don't understand the question."

Terry wanted to get Char alone so they could discuss their strategy. "I think we should take Lucinda for a bathroom break."

"It is not my time," the Erthos replied.

"That's okay. If there's a will, there's a way." Terry

turned Lucinda toward the door. With Terry and Char each taking an elbow, they hurried from the room. A quick left, a wave of the wristband, and they shoved Lucinda through the open door. "Don't come out until we tell you we're ready for you."

When the door closed, Terry was first to blurt what was on his mind.

"What the fuck?"

"I wish I knew," Char replied. "She must have a chip in her brain, but I'm not going to crack her skull to look for it. We'll assume she does and that Claymore is the computer."

"Agreed." Terry started to pace, something he did when deep in thought. He also liked to talk through things, even if only with himself. "Claymore knows things and shares select memories with the reincarnations, but usually shares nothing. Since we've arrived, they've probably gone through more bodies than they've used in hundreds of years.

"Machines that make stuff, same as the *War Axe*. Food that's the best we've ever had. How does it know, and how is it fooling our senses?"

"Maybe it is that good?" Char suggested.

"I can't believe that. It simply knows how to tickle our pleasure centers. Well, mine, anyway. That was the best burger and curly fries I've ever had, or at least I was convinced of it. The burger even looked and smelled exactly like I thought it would."

"Can I come out now?" a voice said from the bathroom.

"Not yet." Char's lips turned white as she pinched her mouth shut, not expanding on Terry's thought.

"Everything goes into the shredder for recycling, so don't use the cleaning bot tunnels. For our own health."

"What's that have to do with anything?" Char wondered.

"That's where my thoughts went after the burger."

"But they have plumbing, too."

"Yes. Plenty of water, it seems, along with plenty of foodstuffs."

"That doesn't answer our main question."

"How do we get out of here?" Terry ventured.

"Then our second main question. How can we talk to Claymore?"

"Claymore will be able to show us the way to the surface. He might be the one giving the orders."

"What if he's related to Ten?" Char didn't look happy thinking about the AI they had chased beyond the frontier and fought at his home base of the ubiquitously named "Homeworld."

"Then we will defeat him like we defeated Ten."

"Ted and Ankh defeated Ten. Aaron and Yanmei defeated Ten. We fought the preliminaries, but they handled the title fight," Char replied, using vernacular that resonated with TH.

"Then we'll have to step up our game. I blew up an engine with us in the room."

"I'm not sure I'd claim that as a victory. Ted was furious."

"It was Ted's fault. He told me to hit it but then failed to mention what 'it' was when there was a shiny thing right in front of me. He can be such a dumbass!"

"He expects people to follow along with his train of thought."

"No one can do that beside Ankh and their AIs."

"Artificial Intelligence. Being an AI doesn't mean they are smart. I'm wearing an old Lucinda wristband, yet it still works. Is there a problem with this AI? What if it's studying us through the mean Erthos woman?"

"Can I come out?" she asked right on cue, almost as if she were listening.

"Fine!" Terry yelled at the closed door. Lucinda opened it and walked through. She looked far different from the person who had gone into the bathroom. She didn't look angry or mean. She looked contrite. Terry had a hard time recognizing the emotion for what it was since he had killed her once and so had Char. Her sneer was forever etched in his mind. It had been the last look on her face when he grabbed for her throat.

But this was a different Lucinda. He had to keep reminding himself of that.

"Help us find a way to leave here. This place isn't for us. We live out there among the stars." Terry pointed to the ceiling.

Lucinda looked up.

"If I help you and you are able to leave, we will be secure once again and won't incur any more damage to our home. The logic is undeniable."

"Thank you, Ms. Spock," Terry said, earning himself a punch in the arm. Char gave him a two-second stink-eye, and he took that as an appropriate comeuppance. "Thank you."

Char didn't know if he was talking to her or Lucinda but accepted it at face value.

"Now we're getting somewhere. Can you have some construction bots meet us at the stairway?" Terry looked hopeful. "We'd love to dig farther. I think we're close, and a mechanical assist would be greatly appreciated."

She nodded but didn't say anything.

Char shrugged, winced and grabbed her head before heading down the corridor, left, then left, and left again...

CHAPTER FOURTEEN

<u>Efluyez Homeworld, Alganor Sector</u>

"I love these helmets," Kai whispered into Christina's ear before giving it a kiss.

"Is that your way of saying you should have gone to Ted first?"

"Maybe, my feisty love muffin."

Christina pushed him away and held him at arm's length. "I'm nobody's love muffin."

"I was... I just... I only..." he stammered.

She cocked one eyebrow and crossed her arms.

"Fuck!" He finally settled on the one-word answer to *all* the universe's problems.

"Now that we know our mutually respectful places, shall we continue?"

Kai grumped and scuffed his boot on the non-skid surface of the hangar bay.

"How many helmets are done, and when will we have them all?"

"One-third. These have technical components we don't

need for this parade, but Ted locked the design so neither Smedley nor I can make any changes." Kai watched the warriors marching in formation. Kimber guided them from a column left—a left turn of row by row—to column left, marking a continuous square on the hangar deck. "If there are no problems, we'll get the final helmet four hours before the parade kicks off."

"One day to show time, and twenty hours until we're ready." Christina chewed her lip for a moment. "I don't like the time crunch."

Kai had no answer for her. The ballistic cloaks had been ready on time, and the helmets were being churned out at the rate of two per hour. There was no way to speed up the process.

Plus, Ted had locked them out of the CIC. They had gotten all they were going to get from their resident genius.

"But they are damn good helmets!" Kai offered. Christina rolled hers over in her hands. Streamlined, integrated heads-up display, and ballistic protection around the head with a secondary piece to cover the wearer's neck. The screen was something neither of them had ever seen before.

"Our ship is capable of making something like this?" Christina asked.

"Ted is capable, but no one else. I need that material structure so we can put it in other things. Maybe in all the things."

Christina gestured for Kimber to take a break.

"Company! Halt," she commanded. The unit came to a

stop, and the warriors remained locked at the position of attention. "Rest in place."

They remained where they were and shook out the aches and tightness from their bodies. The warriors kept their left feet planted so if Kimber called them back to attention, they would immediately assume the tight formation that they had when they stopped.

The Bad Company was going to be parade-ready, and the helmets would be ready in time.

Everything was falling into place, which worried Christina. She started walking toward the formation and Kimber met her halfway.

"Looking good, Kim."

"We've seen the parade field. We've met the lackeys." Kimber threw her hands up in frustration. "Where is an ambush going to come from?"

"I wish I knew." Christina wore a troubled look as she scanned the faces in the formation. If she failed them, warriors would die.

Even with their ballistic cloaks and helmets.

"So we have to be ready for everything. Black Eagles overhead. The *War Axe* ready to crash-dive the planet. Mechs fully armed and weapons-hot with sensor systems working overtime," Christina added.

"If there is anything to see, our people will see it."

"Maybe practice scatter-and-cover?"

"Railguns all the way around, and no matter what the Flayse think, we're going in fully loaded."

"What are the rules of engagement?"

"Isn't that the million-credit question?" Christina

looked back and forth between Kim and the company. "Let's see what our people think."

Together they strolled to the front of the formation, where Kimber brought the company to attention.

Christina took a deep breath and spoke loud enough for all to hear without yelling. "We'll reconvene in the chow hall in fifteen so we can talk about what tomorrow will look like. We only have one chance to get this right. We don't know what's going to happen down there, but we have to be ready for all contingencies."

"We'll rip their fucking heads off and shit down their necks!" someone shouted.

"Yeah! Fuck those asswipes!"

"Bint-hole-sucking, ball-slapping, pustule-infested..."

"Hold on!" Christina yelled into the cacophony of insults. "Who are you going to beat up?"

Silence. Until one lone voice. "The enemy?"

"Yeah!" The insults started afresh.

"SHUT UP!" Christina's eyes started to bulge and veins throbbed in her neck as she fought to stay in control. "We are going down to a parade. We'll be marching. The enemy is hidden, and may never reveal himself. All of a sudden, it could be chaos. Then what? Are you going to shoot some bystanders?"

The big mouths remained shut under Christina's withering glare. She softened and let out a breath she'd been holding.

"We are one of the best and most experienced fighting units in the galaxy. All of you are professionals. This gig is different. I wanted to talk about it over chow, but we'll do it here. You need to know what I know. I don't have the answers, but whatever we do, we're all going to do it together.

"Our contract is to march in their parade and intimidate their neighbors, but they have offered us a ridiculous sum for four hours of our time. We figure there is something more, as in, they are going to use us to start a war with their neighbor, Frikanda. Our best guesstimate is that there is going to be a terrorist attack, and I use the term 'terrorist' loosely. We think the Flayse Conglomerate is going to conduct the attack and frame Frikanda for it.

"So, we have to be ready for an attack from an unknown location using unknown means. We probably won't see our enemy. That's how terrorists work. But we're going to be in the kill zone. That's why the cloaks and helmets. We'll need an immediate response from everyone faster than you've ever reacted before, and we have to move as one. We expect secondary ambushes to be set up on the egress routes.

"I also personally believe that the Flayse are willing to sacrifice their own people to further their goals. How many? The ambitious have no limits on the damage they can do. I want to eliminate the traitorous Flayse at the outset, and we have a plan we're working with Smedley to help us identify some of the possible candidates."

The company continued to listen attentively even though Christina had stopped speaking.

Kim stepped up. "What rules of engagement do we need so we don't kill any innocent bystanders?"

Joseph and Petricia walked forward, helmets in hand. "I volunteer to canvass the crowd, looking for anyone who plans to do us harm."

"I was hoping you would. You'll be our special liaison. Plus, they've already met you. They might flip their lids when they see the mechs, so you'll be far more palatable to the sensitive and peace-loving murderers."

"Have they already killed someone?" Joseph asked, although he already knew the answer.

"No, but they will!"

"What if you're wrong?" he pressed.

"I'm not." Christina set her jaw as if preparing for a fight, but then she relaxed and shook her head. "If nothing happens, we'll take our credits and leave. Nothing would make me happier."

"I don't think you're wrong." Joseph wanted to explore all sides of the potential. "There's something going on. I could hear it and sense it, but I couldn't pin it down."

"So we have to be ready for anything. We'll have our people at the most strategic locations in and around the parade field."

Kimber pointed at nothing, but it drew all eyes to her. "Besides damaging the Bad Company's ego, what would be their best target? How would a terrorist who wanted to start a war with Frikanda do it to get the biggest bang for the buck?"

"I haven't heard that phrase in a long, long time," Joseph quipped. "But it makes sense. They want to hurt us, but only enough to make us angry and entice us to go after the so-called perpetrators."

"I've been thinking about this all wrong," Christina's eyes lit up. "Joseph, you're a genius. Reconvene upstairs in fifteen. I need to check on something."

· · ·

Band Rayal Seven, Okkoto

Terry hurried to catch up. "Are you okay?"

"I have a splitting headache. It's been building. I'm sure it's just being confined down here. I'd say I prefer the open air, but we live on a spaceship and a space station. I still like the green grass of home and getting naked under the sun."

Terry wanted to smile, but despite her words, she had paled and looked to be in pain. She didn't want Terry to worry, which made him worry more.

"I'll handle the heavy lifting. Drink plenty of water and rest," he offered.

"I stand ready to help. There is plenty in there that you can't move by yourself."

Lucinda walked along in silence.

Terry turned to her. "Is the air different down here since we arrived?"

"I don't know," she replied, which was the answer Terry expected. "Maybe we can get Tonie to help us? He seemed well-versed in what was going on around here."

"Tonie Sall-mon?" Lucinda asked.

"Yes."

"No." She shook her head as she spoke. "He won't be of much help."

She continued to walk behind them without offering further explanation.

Terry couldn't let it go. He didn't trust the Erthos, although he believed their goals were aligned. "Why not?"

"He doesn't think like us."

Terry smiled. "Maybe that's why we should ask him.

People who think like you haven't been able to get us out of here. All we want is to leave."

Lucinda didn't reply, remaining stoic in their march to the stairway.

Char perked up as they walked, color returning to her face.

"Time to move some rock," she told him, determined.

"Rock the Casbah." Terry worked his shoulders and arms to get them ready for what he figured would be a hard workout, bordering on a battle. He was in a fight against the rocks. His lip curled as his war face made a brief appearance.

They arrived at the fall without having to fight security bots. Terry hugged the wall, watching for movement. "Are we safe to work?"

"Yes." Lucinda leaned against the wall and crossed her arms.

Char looked at Terry's sour expression. "You didn't expect her to get her hands dirty, did you?"

Terry thought about it for a moment. "Probably not in your job description, is it?" he asked before digging into the pile, moving what he could before enlisting Char's help to leverage larger chunks of stone.

They made great progress over the next two hours before Char sat down, rubbing her temples. Terry shined his flashlight in crevices and cracks, looking for any sign of an opening beyond. All he could see was that it grew more densely packed. There would be no going over the top. The ceiling had become one with a boulder that wouldn't be removed.

"Unless we blow it," Terry muttered, more to himself than Char.

"The laser pistol won't cut it."

He realized he'd spoken aloud when he stopped and turned. "Explosives." He climbed down and wiped the sweat from his face with the back of his sleeve. "Lucinda, is there a lab where we might find nitrates for fertilization? And a few other things we'll need to set up a nice blast to help us clear this mess."

"No," she said.

Terry fought the urge to grab her and shake her. "We need to take a break and get some chow. Have to keep the engine fueled." Terry patted his stomach. "And maybe a shower. Where can I get a shower?"

"Follow me," Lucinda said resignedly.

Terry wrapped his arm around Char's waist as she shuffled after the Erthos leader. He found that he was mostly supporting her and stopped to look at her face. Her eyes were unfocused and her breath ragged.

"What's wrong?" he asked, giving her a small shake. "Char?"

"Head. Migraine."

"I need to get you someplace to rest. Lots of water. Lucinda?" The Erthos was gone. "I fucking hate these people."

Char chuckled softly before her eyes rolled back in her head and she collapsed. Terry caught before she dropped.

"Sorry, Tonie, I'm kicking you out of your room," Terry muttered as he lifted Char into his arms and started to run. After turning the first corner, he collided with Lucinda.

"I wondered where you went. What's wrong with her?" She looked at Char's limp body.

"We need to get her into a bed to rest. I'm heading for Tonie's room unless you have a better idea."

"Follow me," Lucinda said, and began walking at a leisurely pace.

"Hurry the fuck up," Terry growled. She gave him a stony gaze while maintaining her same pace. When they reached the dining room, she opened the door and gestured for them to enter.

"You have got to be shitting me," he said. Lucinda shrugged. "The more you dissemble, the longer you will have us around. The longer I'm here, the more likely it will be that I start fucking your shit up. We've already killed you twice, or maybe it's three times. I've lost count."

Terry laid Char on the table and took the laser pistol from her waistband. He pointed it at Lucinda. Her expression and willingness to work with them had grown decidedly colder throughout their time together. Terry wondered where he'd gone wrong in leveraging her to help them.

He decided to ignore the Erthos and rushed to the food processor, ordering a liter of warm water. It delivered within seconds, and Terry hurried back to his wife. He cradled her head as he dribbled water on her lips. She smacked them slowly.

"Take a drink, Char. I'll hold the water. Open up, and I'll pour it slowly," he said, trying to minister to her. In their long lives, they'd never been sick. They had been injured to the point of near death, but once through the worst, the nanos saved them. Terry didn't know what to do since she wasn't getting better.

He helped her with the first drink and then others until she'd downed half the container. After that, she was able to sit up.

"I must have been dehydrated or something," she said slowly, slurring some of the words.

"We don't get dehydrated," Terry replied.

"Or something," Bethany Anne added.

"Jesus! You scared the shit out of me," Terry said after his initial jump. "Welcome back, by the way."

"Where's your ménage partner?"

"My what?" Terry looked past BA and saw that Lucinda had disappeared. "Sonofabitch."

"You need to get your bitches under control, is what I'm seeing. If they tried that on me? Asses would get kicked. Why are you sitting on the table?" BA eyed Char.

"A little under the weather," Char replied.

"Bullshit." BA leaned close. Terry ventured a hand toward her. "Stop." She threw a wink in his direction. "Nutsack out your mouth. Did you forget about that?"

"Nothing." Terry failed at trying to look innocent.

"That's some leg-humping nipple-pipe you have going on there. TH, you need to get this woman out of here right now."

Terry's mouth fell open and he grunted.

"What the fuck was that?"

"Trying to get out of here is the only thing I've been doing since we dropped into this cesspool!"

She stood up. "Stop trying and start *doing*."

Terry's shoulders slumped, and he held Char close as he looked down.

"Are you giving up?"

"I'm regrouping for a final assault by overwhelming force on Band Rayal Seven. I need to find Tonie and drag him around until he tells me something I want to hear."

BA tapped her foot while she stood in her power pose, legs shoulder-width apart and tapping her finger to her lips before waving toward the door. "You better get going. I'll stay here with Charumati. We have plenty to talk about."

"If you stay with us out there," Char interjected, "I could tag along. I feel better with you here."

Bethany Anne looked down. "That's because I'm holding back most of the Etheric energy that is eating away at you like acid on metal. We'll stay right here." She looked over to TH. "Put on your running shoes and get going. If I pop out of here again, Char gets an unfiltered onslaught. If the Etheric kills her, there's *no* coming back from it."

His brows narrowed. "How did she handle it until now?"

"Do you want answers or Char's life?" She pointed to the door. "Don't be a dumbass."

Terry didn't say another word, just waved his wristband to open the door and bolted through. He passed Lucinda, who was carrying a blanket and pillow.

"Good! She's in there." Terry pointed with his thumb over his shoulder as he ran for the power room, where he hoped to find Tonie.

CHAPTER FIFTEEN

<u>Mess Deck on the *War Axe*</u>

Christina looked at the Bad Company's leadership – vampires, weretigers, and nano-boosted. A thousand years of experience in that one small group. She wanted to bring all of it to bear.

"What if it's the Frikandans?" Christina asked.

"Why would they want us to march in the Flayse parade?" Kimber asked.

"They said the purpose was to intimidate their neighbors," Christina replied. "What if that was all true? Who would be able to do something with that information?"

"Someone trying to unseat the Magnate?" Petricia offered. Christina tapped her nose, showing she thought that was one possibility.

"The Frikandans," Joseph added.

"By badly trying to stitch up the Frikandans, we turn our weapons on the Flayse Conglomerate, when it might have been the Frickers in the first place." Christina looked like she had a more complete answer but didn't share.

"That puts us back to square one," Kimber said, making it a question.

"A diplomatic counterattack to foil the terrorists without taking sides, so no matter who is responsible, both sides will be forced to the table."

Joseph nodded. "'Forced' being the operative word here."

"We don't protect ourselves. We protect the dignitaries—the Magnate and his people, and the Frikandans and their entourage. Then we stuff them in a room together and keep them from killing each other," Christina explained.

"A good offense is the best defense," Auburn added. He usually spoke very little, but when he did, it was a critical observation. Since he was named after a football team following the World's Worst Day Ever, he'd had a forced indoctrination into all things related to his father's passion. The analogy seemed to fit.

The others agreed.

"Occam's Razor," Joseph remarked. "The principle by which the easiest answer is most likely the correct one. We waste no time trying to figure out who did it or spin our wheels coming up with complex theories. In the end, the only thing that matters is that we finish this war, even if it hasn't started yet."

"End it once and for all," Kimber declared.

"We will break the company into combat action teams with overlapping responsibilities to seize and protect the VIPs. Brief your people. Put Cap and Kelly in mechs, and have them pick two additional since I want four – one on each corner of our formation. Joseph and Petricia will be trolling the crowd gathering intel and showing the flag. First platoon has the Flayse and Second platoon has the Frikandans. The four-legged platoon will be carrying additional heavy weapons under their cloaks, and they'll march at the back of the formation."

"The four-legged platoon only has three warriors," Kimber noted.

"They're our heavy weapons. Biggest bang for the buck, right?" Christina closed her eyes as she viewed the parade ground in her mind's eye. "Detail a squad from Second Platoon to fall in on the heavy weapons to assist Bundin, K'Thrall, and Slikira."

Kimber took charge as Christina stepped back. She checked the time. Her plan had now become so complex that it required more practice time than they had, but practice they would, until the last second.

Band Rayal Seven, Okkoto

Terry ran down the empty corridors, his footfalls pounding a steady beat. He waved his wristband in front of Tonie's door, but it didn't open. *Recoded it. He's the only smart one down here,* Terry thought.

He pounded on the door, as Tonie had done before putting his ear to it. No sounds from within. He hammered on it again. Still nothing. Terry bolted for the room at the end of the corridor, satisfied when it opened for him.

"You!" Tonie complained. "Haven't you done enough damage?"

"My wife is dying," Terry explained, "thanks to the

abundance of Etheric energy being pumped into this place. I need you to throttle it back or help us get out of here."

"I didn't hear the option I'm going to select, which is do nothing."

"You sound more like us than any of these other drones. Lucinda doesn't like you because of it." Terry moved closer to the Erthos so the sincerity of his next statement would be unmistakable. "If my wife dies, I will wreak havoc on this place. I will crush your cloning machines beneath my feet. I will turn every one of your hydroponics labs into an unrecoverable wasteland. At the end of the day, no one will know you ever existed, and I won't care if I die while doing it. Believe this to be the truth as much as you believe any other fact you may embrace."

"I'm still going to do nothing." Tonie crossed his arms and jutted his chin with his defiance, but his expression had softened. "You seem to be the threat guy. Always threatening."

"I don't want to be that guy, but sometimes I'm impatient when I need stuff to happen. I'm the get-it-done guy."

"Are you getting it done now?"

Terry smiled and hung his head. He was ready to kill this Tonie to see if a new one would be more tractable but thought he'd try one last desperate attempt. "Please?"

"If it'll get you out of here quicker, then I guess it'll be okay." Tonie moved to the main control panel. Terry joined him, even though he couldn't make any sense of the buttons and screens. "This is for the main shield that hides our existence." He pointed to a screen at the top that was a single color. There were no ways to adjust any of it.

"These controls are for everything else within the

complex." Tonie waved his hand over the rest of the panel. "Let's cut out all of manufacturing and production. We'll change it to night mode across the board, reducing power to the hydroponics bays to a minimum. Environmental control is restricted and all manufacturing ceases, so don't kill anyone. We can't bring their clone to life while we're in night mode." Tonie pointed to the panel before turning to Terry Henry. "There! An eighteen percent reduction in power consumption."

"That's it?" Terry asked.

Tonie's smile evaporated, and he glared at the human.

"The Etheric shield is seventy percent of our power usage, and that is a standard figure. We can't affect it."

"You could if you shut down the generators."

"I knew you were a crazy man! I could tell by the look in your eyes," Tonie accused.

"Hear me out. The shields can't use more power than is generated. Feed them, just less. I expect the shields will adjust, or I may get to meet the AI running this nuthouse."

"The who is running what?" Tonie wondered. He dragged his fingers through his hair and contemplated the problem. Terry stood there as if rooted to the floor. The big human wasn't going anywhere until Tonie satisfied his demands. "Let's give it a whirl and see what we come up with."

Tonie moved to a second panel that didn't appear to have an interface and removed the cover to show the controls hidden beneath. He looked up at Terry Henry, who nodded, and back at the panel.

"Here goes nothing—or my life. We've never done this

before, so it could be quite catastrophic." He tapped a few of the buttons, holding his breath as he listened.

"Shield is down to thirty percent."

"I hope that's enough—" Terry started.

They heard the low rumble at the same time. It reverberated through their feet before it ended with a vigorous shake of the walls. It slowed and returned back to their feet before disappearing.

"What the hell just happened?" Terry asked.

"*You* happened," Tonie replied. "I was here, same as you. How would I know what happened?"

"I thought the shield was there to hide this facility. I didn't expect it to handle structural integrity."

"It is there to keep us safe. Are all humans this dense? I would like to study your species, but I'd probably get bored as you tried to figure out how to make tools."

"I'd say that I like you so I'll kill you last, but that line is overused. I don't care what you think about me, just help us get the fuck out of here. Now, can you get the elevator to us?"

"Of course not!" Tonie declared, exasperated. "Night mode." He shook his head and rolled his eyes. "Do you want the Etheric energy to work or not? Elevator needs energy. No energy, wife happy, no elevator."

"You're beginning to sound like Ted. Chill. With the power off, you've bought us some time. You can turn on the elevator from here?"

"No," he said softly, and winced under Terry's withering gaze.

"So you're talking out your ass, trying to sound smart. You're just being a dick to be a dick." Terry grabbed the

Erthos and threw him toward the door. "You're going to take me to the place where the elevator can be controlled."

"Maybe we should find out what that rumble was first?"

"I don't care what that rumble was. I want the elevator, and I want it right fucking now."

"You'll care about the rumble when you see what caused it," Tonie countered.

Terry kept his hand on the Erthos' shoulder. "Now you're back to being a dick, right when I thought we had an understanding." Terry shook Tonie, then shook him again. "Better now?"

"Stop doing that or I won't help you."

"Stop being a dick to me, or I'll kill you and we'll see if the next Tonie is a little nicer."

"Manufacturing is off because of night mode. There won't be another Tonie."

"Here's what I think. Night mode is only temporary, and the power will come back on after a certain amount of time has passed. For the generators you turned off, they won't come back to life, so maybe you're right. We might not come out of night mode since all the power is funneled to the shield. The bottom line is an unhelpful Tonie and a dead Tonie both have the exact same value to me, except I don't have to wonder if a dead Tonie will stab me in the back."

Tonie kept his gaze steady. He didn't back down, but he was no match for Terry Henry Walton.

"It appears that we have reached a mutually beneficial arrangement, then. I prefer not to have this version of me terminated. Can you stop threatening me now?"

"Yes." Terry settled on a one-word answer, no further

explanation required. He wouldn't threaten the Erthos engineer. If he put Char's life at risk, Terry would take care of him. No words needed. "Where is the other control room, the one for the elevator?"

"It's near the elevator, but the lock-out sequence needs to be overridden. That control room is on the far side of Band Rayal Seven."

"Then we better get going before anything else happens." Terry opened the door, and the two hurried out. When they reached the four-way intersection, they discovered what had caused the rumble.

The corridor leading back to the dining area and the elevator was filled with rock that used to be the ceiling.

"Is there another way?" Terry asked, eyes fixed on the obstruction.

"Yes, but it's the long way around."

"No time to waste, Tonie."

The Erthos took a left and started running but stopped. Terry dodged to the side before holding his hands up, questioning why they weren't moving.

"I need to activate a remote so we can turn the generators back on. That's what it will take to move the elevator."

He ran past Terry, heading back from the way they'd come.

Stop wasting time, Terry thought, clenching his teeth so tightly that the muscles in his cheeks bulged and his jaw began to ache.

Terry easily kept pace with the Erthos on their way to the power control room. Once inside, Tonie touched a few controls and then leaned back in thought. Terry rolled his finger, hoping the signal might encourage Tonie to hurry.

It didn't.

After a couple of minutes, Tonie smacked a fist into his palm. "I'll need to set them to auto-start. We need to have everything ready to go by then. Otherwise, I'm sorry."

"How long will it take us to go around?"

"I've never done it. It's a few karascals through the support bot tunnels."

"How far is a karascal?"

Tonie opened the door and looked down the residential corridor. "That's about one-tenth of a karascal."

"I'd say that's a hundred meters, so say a kilometer. We have to crawl for a few kilometers?" Terry was taken aback. "Better give us a couple hours at least."

"An hour? I'll figure out what it would take me. Calculating," Tonie said as if he were a computer. "Okay. I'll triple the estimate because I know me, and I'm going to get tired. As long as our power is as low as possible, I hope that relieves the pressure on your wife. It will have to. There is no other course of action."

Tonie jogged out the door and ran at a measured pace, saving his energy for the grind to come.

"If you want to leave with us, we can show you what's out there. It's a big universe," Terry suggested.

"I've read some information on it. It's dangerous."

"If people like me can survive out there, why don't you think you can?"

"You have a good point. Has engineering advanced?" he asked.

Terry smiled. "It had to be set back first, all the way to the Stone Age, but we're leaping forward now. I'm sure you'd learn a thing or two."

Tonie was already breathing hard when they hit the end of the long corridor. The Erthos motioned to the left, and they went toward the side of the complex, the part Terry and Char had not yet explored.

"Why would you ask me to go with you? You've already threatened to kill me multiple times. I have no desire to live under constant threat."

"I get aggressive when dealing with uncooperative aliens who jerk me around. For what it's worth, I apologize. I won't do it again. I only want to save my wife."

"I see." Tonie didn't say more, saving his breath for running. They reached the end of another corridor and took a right before reaching another corner where they turned left, leading farther away from the cave in and Char.

Terry wanted to ask Tonie if this was the right way but decided the question and answer would be meaningless. They were going where they were going regardless. Terry didn't know of anything else to do.

When the corridor dead-ended, Tonie swiped his wristband to access a side-room. The space was empty, but Tonie walked to the wall and kicked open the hidden door that gave the cleaning bots access. "Now for the hard part."

CHAPTER SIXTEEN

The _War Axe_, in orbit over the Efluyez Homeworld, Alganor Sector

The warriors shuffled out of formation on their way to their rooms.

"Sleep fast," she said softly to their backs. She was tired too, but in four hours they'd be back here on the hangar deck, ready to board the six drop ships—the Pods that would take them to the planet surface.

If the _War Axe_ dropped them off, the Bad Company's Direct Action Branch would be left without transportation. If the shit hit the fan, egress always made for a viable tactic, unless there were no Pods to carry them. The new plan kept the _War Axe_ in low orbit from the outset.

Weapons hot, just in case the terrorists pulled out some heavy firepower of their own. The _War Axe_ was heavier, and with her overhead, no one on Efluyez would risk her wrath in a straight-up fight.

"Dokken? What are you doing here?" Christina asked after the hangar bay had cleared, leaving her alone in the massive space. She used that time to collect her thoughts and prepare for the next day, or in this case, so she would be at the top of her game for the rest of the fight.

I'm going down with you, the German Shepherd told her.

"I can't put you in harm's way, buddy. You have a different job now, and if I got you hurt, Terry Henry would have my ass, no matter who my dad is."

Cory is coming, too, the dog told her as if she hadn't just rejected his plan.

"Cory?" Christina called, expecting her to be waiting in the shadows after sending Dokken to soften her up.

She's sleeping to be ready and alert when the drop ships launch.

"I feel like I should have a say in this," Christina said, knowing that Cory would do what needed to be done. She wasn't coming to be an observer, but to be the Bad Company's medic. She was worried that there would be a fight and people would get hurt. She would use her special skills, the nanocytes that were a gift from her parents Terry and Char that enabled her to use the power of the Etheric to treat wounds and injuries.

"Make sure you both have ballistic cloaks and helmets. Do whatever you have to do to get something that will cover those ears of yours."

You don't make fun of Cory's ears.

Cordelia Dawn was a rare gift delivered to a werewolf and a normal father, but she hadn't gotten the abilities of her mother or her father. She could not change into a werewolf, but she did have wolf's ears, an external manifestation from Char's nano-modified DNA. Cory covered them expertly with long hair when off the ship visiting other places and other races to prevent questions that she wouldn't answer.

"Not poking fun at her, but you, my hairy friend. You are much milder than your sire. Ashur treated giving lip to me as an art form."

Dear old Dad. Can I talk to him? I would like that.

"I don't know where he is, Dokken. As soon as this mission wraps up, we'll look into reuniting you with your family. I'll find out his location through my parents, and we'll figure out a way to make it happen."

I would like that, Dokken repeated.

"When Kai is back in the supply shack, both of you get ballistic cloaks and helmets. For now? I'm hitting the rack."

Supply shack?

"The office at the front of the manufacturing space next to the maintenance area."

Why didn't you just say that? Humans are so obtuse.

"*There's* your dad!" Christina declared. "Supply shack, three hours. Don't be late. If you don't get your cloaks and helmets, I can't let you go to the planet surface."

We'll be there. We have to be there, Dokken replied.

Band Rayal Seven, Okkoto

Terry pulled himself forward through the crawlspace, having to wait for Tonie, who would crawl for a minute and then rest for a minute. Terry shined his flashlight ahead to provide light for both of them. Tonie wasn't able to crawl and carry the flashlight.

"Let me take the lead. You can hang on, and I'll pull you." Terry tried to sound encouraging, but he was desperate. He wanted to get to the control panel and then to the elevator before the systems kicked on and returned full power.

Etheric energy rushing in like a tidal wave to consume Char.

"Please," Terry begged.

"At the next intersection, I'll wedge to the side, and you crawl ahead," Tonie panted.

Terry was ready to scream by the time they reached that next intersection. He guessed that it had taken more than an hour to crawl a couple hundred meters—or it could have been ten minutes. The outpost had thrown off his internal clock so much that he didn't know which way was up. All he knew was that his body was raging for a resolution. He needed to be doing something to fix the problem.

It went to the core of his being. He couldn't sit back while others cured the galaxy's ills. Char was sick, and he needed to get her out of this place. Tonie was the key, but he was also an anchor. Terry was going to drag the anchor to the lock and Tonie was going to open it.

Terry tried not to focus on the fact that Tonie could have done all that days ago before any of their problems began, but he had not cared to help the strangers back then.

Do people need a crisis in order to act? Terry thought before noting more examples from history than he could catalog. His famous eidetic memory pulled facts and figures from the books he'd read. *Yes, they do.*

When the way ahead cleared, Terry surged forward, stopping when he was abreast of the Erthos. Tonie had thrown himself into the side tunnel. He was curled up and looked like he was asleep except for his labored breathing.

"Are you okay, buddy?" Terry asked.

"Yes. Just. Need. Rest." A full breath between words. Tonie was on his last legs, and time was running out.

"Grab my ankles and hang on." Terry moved ahead and waited for an agonizingly long time before Tonie gripped an ankle with one hand, then the other. Terry had assumed the Erthos would take one foot with each hand, but with only one leg encumbered, it would be easier to crawl.

And more importantly, make up for lost time.

Terry powered forward. "Make sure you tell me when to turn. Backtracking would suck massive muddy moose balls."

"I'll take your word for it." Tonie grunted with each pull. "Keep going straight for another karascal and then we'll take a right, then a left. After that, any access tunnel to your right will take you into a room that's beyond the fall. Unless there was a second collapse."

"Don't even think things like that. Don't even..." Terry let the thought hang as he focused on the only thing he could do, which was to move forward. Get to a place where they could stand upright and cover the distance in seconds instead of minutes.

Tonie lost his grip only three times over the next kilometer, but Terry could hear the Erthos' struggles and suffering.

"We'll be there soon, my man," Terry said, continuing his forward motion. Pull with his arms, push with his leg. Pull. Push. "Let me tell you a story about Ted. I used to discount anything he had to say because he was thinking so far over my head that we had nothing in common. I needed that which I could use right then, but Ted was thinking about things like perpetual power. When I finally listened, Ted helped bring nuclear power to a destroyed world."

Pull. Push. Corner up ahead.

"All we had to do was give him the tools to work his magic. Only Gene, a werebear, understood the engineering like Ted, but in the end, they made it happen. And Ted didn't rest on his laurels. He didn't sit back and bask in the glory of his success. He looked for bigger and bigger challenges. Do you know what he just engineered?"

Tonie grunted, tapped Terry's leg to get his attention, and pointed to the right. A few more pulls, then drag them both around the corner.

"He figured out a way to use Etheric energy to power an instantaneous universal communication system. That's right. We can talk to a planet ten thousand light years away in real time. Ted has a gift, and we just needed to listen to him."

"Was it so hard to give him a chance?" Tonie asked as they rested for a moment while working their way through the four-way tunnel intersection.

"It was, because there were too few of us to meet too many demands, but when we could spare the time, we learned how to increase our productivity exponentially. As an engineer, you can appreciate that. Orders of magnitude greater return once the investment price was paid."

"I would like the freedom to do something different. Maybe I *will* join you when you leave." Tonie's breathing had slowed but his face still glistened, his eyes red from sweat dripping into them. At least there wasn't any dust.

"My compliments on your air handling system. If you could scrub our air this clean to keep the dust and dirt from settling, you'd be worth your weight in gold."

"What is my weight in gold?" Tonie shook his head. "Never mind. It doesn't matter. We are close now. Let's get out of these ducts, Terry Henry."

"TH to my friends, and I couldn't agree more." Terry turned and started to crawl with renewed vigor. After another four hundred meters, various cross tunnels started to appear. He took the first left, and two hundred meters later, took a right and pulled himself toward the small door that opened into a normal space beyond.

Terry didn't hesitate. He pushed the door open and crawled through. He rose quickly to his feet and froze. Tonie struggled through the opening, pushing on one of Terry's legs so he could get by.

"Security robots," Terry whispered, but Tonie forced his way through by poking Terry in the calf until he moved his leg.

"So?" Tonie said when he stood up. "Let's go." He walked around the two security bots pointing their laser pistols and opened the door.

Terry took one step and the bots opened fire.

The War Axe

"I don't think I could be more tired. Tireder? Tiredest?" Kai ventured while cradling his mug of food-processor coffee. Cory looked chipper as she waited for him to deliver the cloaks for her and Dokken. The German Shepherd stood next to her, wagging his tail slowly but regularly.

He yawned before standing and walking into the back where the production processes took place. The stocking shelves were empty, but an automated tracking robot held two cloaks and one helmet. He took them, leaving the bot empty-handed and waiting for one last item—Dokken's helmet.

"Here you go, Aunt Cory. Make sure it all fits, but at this point, there's not much we can do if it doesn't."

Cory, as she always did, took care of Dokken before herself. She draped the cloak over his back. It didn't have a strap under his belly to hold it in place. His tail brushed it back and forth until it hung askew.

"We need a modification," Cory told her nephew, but Kai had balanced his face on his hand and was out cold while hunched over his desk. "It looks like it's up to you and me to remedy the situation."

Cory started to leave, but Dokken stopped her. *Have you tried on yours yet?*

"I'm sure it'll fit."

It'll take ten seconds, and I'll feel so much better, Dokken said. His telepathic voice suggesting he wouldn't take no for an answer.

Cory balanced her helmet on the dog's back, which made him stand still. She threw the cloak around her shoulders and clasped it at her neck. "This will be all the fashion after people see it!" she quipped. The helmet rested lightly on her head, wedged against her protruding wolf ears but still allowed for clear vision both front and peripheral. She activated the HUD, but the helmet wasn't linked with any collection systems and gave her a null information screen.

"It works. Any exposed flesh?" she asked.

Dokken walked around her before nodding his approval. *It will protect you,* he said before adding, *I shudder to think what my helmet will look like.*

"It'll be the height of fashion!" she declared. "Let's fix that miscue with a strap. All we have is duct tape."

No! You are not duct-taping me. Dokken pranced in agitation.

"I'm not going to tape *you,* just your cloak. At least let me show you what I'm thinking." She bent down, but Dokken bolted into the hangar bay. His cloak slipped farther sideways until he tripped over it and face-planted across the non-skid decking. He stood gingerly, his face bleeding from where his lip had gotten cut.

Cory grabbed his dog face, and her nanos started to glow blue beneath her hands.

Save that for the injured warriors! He tried to pull away, but she held him tightly.

"I will do as I please, mister. You're injured and you're a warrior, so stand still." She continued to hold him while the blue glowed faintly beneath her fingers. "I'll be there when they need me."

CHAPTER SEVENTEEN

Band Rayal Seven, Okkoto

Terry charged the closest bot, wrapping it in his arms and picking it up. The thing hammered on his back until he dumped it into the other. He drove his legs, ignoring the pain in his chest and arms from the brief but multiple laser burns.

With one final heave, Terry forced the two bots over. He scrambled to pull the laser pistol from one while standing on the metal wrist of the other. The bots were tangled together, but Terry couldn't free the pistol from the metal monster's grip. He twisted and pulled, to no avail.

He looked frantically around for anything he could use as a weapon, finally settling on his own Ka-bar. He pulled with his off-hand and jammed it into a seam in the top security bot's chest. The one beneath continued to flail harmlessly as long as Terry stood on its wrist.

Starting to lose his balance, he pulled the knife and let his weight fall on it as he jammed it into a neck seam. He forced his weight onto the pommel and bounced while working the knife back and forth. The bot sparked, and a bolt of lightning shot from it. Terry was lifted into the air and came down in a heap beside the bots.

He grunted through the pain. He saw his knife still wedged in the thing's neck, the leather-wrapped handle smoking slightly. Terry got to his knees just in time for the dead bot to get thrown into his face, and he batted it aside. Had he been standing, it probably would have knocked him down.

Terry lunged forward, grabbing the dropped laser pistol as he hit the remaining security bot just below its mechanical waist. He kept pushing until they ran into the wall, then shoved the laser pistol against the metal of the thing's torso and fired. He kept the trigger down until the beam burst with a splatter of molten metal from the mechanical shoulder. Terry stopped and fell back from the new burns on his face.

He blinked his good eye and fired again into the bot's chest, but it was already starting to topple. Terry stepped back and the second dead bot fell at his feet. "Son of a mother-fuck," Terry complained. His nanos were already hard at work repairing the horrendous injuries he'd sustained. Terry limped to the first bot he'd killed and yanked his Ka-bar from it, stuffing it back into its sheath.

Terry collected the second laser pistol, wishing his nanos would heal his eyeball since he could only see out of the one. It was messing with his depth perception.

"I've never seen anything like that," Tonie said softly. "So violent, but invigorating!"

"Invigorating," Terry mumbled. "I forgot to tell you that

we want the boring route to the chow hall, not the exciting one."

"That shouldn't have happened. You're with me, and you're wearing my wristband."

"Didn't you recode your wristband?"

"Oh. I'm sorry about that. Finding a dead body in my shower was more than I could take. You made me angry."

"I'm sorry, too." Terry took off the tainted wristband and threw it onto the dead robot.

"Can you teach me how to fight?" Tonie said, walking into the room and going through the motions of recreating the fight—Terry's charge, using one bot as a shield, killing it, and then focusing on the final one. "Fight one opponent at a time. So much smarter than you look."

"Divide and conquer, bitch," Terry told him. "Come on, the clock is winding down."

"Next stop, elevator control." Tonie offered his shoulder and Terry wrapped an appreciative arm over it. Together they lumbered into the corridor and off to their next target.

The *War Axe*

Christina trooped the line, reviewing the formation for uniformity and attention to detail. The six drop ships stood with doors open on both sides of the hangar bay. The Bad Company's Direct Action Branch stood at attention in the middle. Forty-six warriors stood with their cloaks tight around their bodies and helmets shining, the mirrored front screens giving nothing away of each warrior's face.

Four armored warriors stood at the corners of the formation. The mechanized platoon. Mechs on parade. Christina slapped the heavy front armor of Kelly's rig as she walked by.

"And the broke-dicks," she said to the four-legged warriors. K'Thrall's helmet was grossly oversized to encompass his mandibles. Bundin's helmet was comically elongated to cover a fair part of his stalk-like head. Slikira looked normal except for the oversized boat cloak. She made the shield on her helmet transparent so Christina could see her smile.

"Show me," Christina ordered.

They pulled their cloaks aside to reveal the weapons beneath. Between the lot of them, they had two anti-armor rocket launchers with eight total reloads, four heavy rail-guns, and two mortars.

"Mortars?" Christina wondered.

"In case an enemy is hiding behind bleachers or somewhere direct weapons can't fire. We'll have to have an observer, but the mechs have mini-drones they can launch for target acquisition. We'll be fine. If we have to fire them, we'll do it without causing collateral damage," Bundin explained.

"I like the way you think, Corporal. Carry on," she told him. Christina headed back into the formation, unable to tell one warrior from the next. She returned to the front of the formation, where she removed her own helmet.

"Weapons," she said in a normal voice. The warriors popped their railguns off their shoulders, twisted the butts, and snapped them down to smack into their left hands.

As one. A single pop and snap reverberated through the

hangar bay. Joseph and Petricia stood in the back of the formation, nodding approvingly at the precision. Christina was pleased with the professional facade the Bad Company had built.

But it wasn't a facade. It was discipline and execution of orders. One team in harmony.

"Scatter!" she yelled, and the precision continued. They broke into smaller groups and raced in all directions, bringing their weapons to bear on imaginary targets while others hurried to grab imaginary VIPs and shield them with their bodies as they moved them to the Pods. Aaron and Yanmei clapped from where they stood in their flight suits by their Black Eagle space fighters.

"Recover!" Christina ordered, and those who had secured heavy weapons from the four-legged warriors returned them before falling back into formation. "At ease."

Kimber had been in formation with the others. She removed her helmet and joined the colonel out front.

"Ready as we're going to be," Kimber whispered.

Christina nodded and held her hands up to silence the warriors. "When I give the command to fall out, you'll board your assigned drop ship and prepare to depart for the planet's surface. When we arrive on the parade deck, you'll immediately form up in marching order. The mechs and our four-legged warriors are our heavy artillery, the king of battle.

"We'll march until either I or Major Kimber gives the word. At that point, we will secure the dignitaries and move them securely to the drop ships, where we will immediately dust off, returning to the *War Axe* when all hands are accounted for. Do not get left behind, and small unit leaders, *do not* leave your people behind.

"We have no idea what the triggering event will be, if any. If there is nothing, we finish the parade, march back to the drop ships, and get the hell out of Dodge. I heard that Colonel Walton had secured some libations for the post-operation party. We will have a total blowout when we return, assuming we don't lose anyone, and that will be a more somber affair. But I don't *want* somber, people! I want a real fucking party with too-loud music, raucous dancing, and a little drinking. To the warrior who gets himself fucked up down on the planet and harshes my party buzz, you are going to be in deep shit. The deepest of shits.

"So don't. As much as your smiling faces make me want to puke, I want to see all of you right back here, ripping off your cloaks and helmets and heading for a shower and hot chow. Anything else will be unacceptable. Don't fuck this up! Fall out!"

The warriors jogged in an orderly manner to the six drop ships. The mechs squeezed in first because if they froze, they'd block everyone from getting out. That was the hard lesson they had learned on Tissikinnon Four. It seemed that all of their procedures were based on experience written in blood. Kimber clapped Christina on the back.

"Long live the Bad Company."

Christina gave Kimber the Spock Hand. "Glory to the warriors."

Joseph and Petricia strolled close on their way to their designated shuttle. "Ready or not, here we come. I don't know what to hope for," Joseph admitted. "I think this would be a great test of the warriors' mettle, but I don't want to see anyone get hurt for a cause that's just stupid."

"We seem to excel in getting hired by the deranged." Christina gave a half-shrug and wished them well.

"They have the most money?" Joseph called over his shoulder as he and Petricia broke into a run, jumping on the ramp as it started to close and boarding last.

Cory jogged by with Dokken by her side. The dog's helmet's face shield was set to transparent instead of the default mirror, and he turned his head and made a face.

"Did you stick your tongue out at me, Private?" Christina called after him. Cory laughed until she boarded.

"At least morale is good," Christina mumbled. "Terry Henry and his damn leadership *thing*. I used to be the one sticking my tongue out. Now they're doing it to me. When did I get old?"

"Never," Kai said from the doorway leading to the maintenance bay. He'd heard her, but then he was modified by the nanos and had ultra-sensitive hearing. "I can't wait to party with you when you get home."

Home. The big gray suck. Who would have thought that? But it is my home now.

When the six Pods were loaded and the ramps secured, Christina contacted the *War Axe*. "Smedley, all hands on deck?"

"All hands are accounted for."

"Launch the drop ships."

Micky started issuing orders to his warship. "Take us into the upper atmosphere, maximum acceleration. Skip once and launch the Pods."

The *War Axe* nosed over and dove toward the planet, pulling up with the first buffeting. Six drop ships launched from the lateral tubes simultaneously and began their descent in a two by three formation. As the heavy destroyer climbed toward a higher orbit, two Black Eagles raced out the open hangar bay door, turned, and fell in behind the Pods carrying the entirety of the Bad Company's Direct Action Branch.

Christina was in the number-one Pod, planned to be the first to touch down. Kimber was in the last Pod to land. That was the plan, anyway.

The *War Axe's* AI had subroutines running on all the drop ships. Smedley was flying the Pods while they were in contact, and his essence would continue the mission if they lost the continuous comm link.

Christina studied the main screen and watched a cloud of ships lift off from the surface and rise toward the Bad Company. Christina tapped the control panel. "Black Eagles, are you seeing what I'm seeing?"

"I expect you're talking about the incoming ships. We'll check them out," Yanmei replied. She was the better pilot of the two weretigers. Aaron was too tall and had a difficult time in the cockpit. He was getting better with practice, but Yanmei was a natural and had been a pilot for a long, long time.

The sleek fighters accelerated past the six drop ships and continued burning toward the lower atmosphere where a light aircraft waited.

"Weapons tight," Christina ordered. "Fire *only* if fired upon."

"Roger," the fighter pilots confirmed. They cycled

through their passive targeting systems, satisfied that they could respond almost as fast as if they were in a weapons-hot status.

Sonic cracks followed them down as they started to spiral to foil enemy targeting systems. When they gained sight of the target, they relaxed.

"Your welcoming committee is ready for your arrival," Yanmei reported. "Every news station and reporter is airborne and waiting for your ships to pass."

"Keep your eyes on them in case there's a lurker in there with some anti-aircraft missiles, although looking at the images you're sending, I don't see anything heavy enough to challenge us."

Yanmei and Aaron throttled back to make a much slower pass. Still, they were traveling at ten times the speed of the light aircraft. Barely more than drones, their purpose was to capture video from on high. The Black Eagles raced by, turned and made a second pass through the area to chase away those who had infringed on the drop ships' flight path.

Aaron laughed softly over the comm link as the light aircraft panicked, bolting in random directions and creating more strife as every plane fought to keep from colliding with its airborne fellows.

Christina tapped the controls to open the ship-to-ship system. "Listen up, people. We are already under scrutiny. We start earning our money right now. Smedley, tighten up this formation. I want geometric perfection on the descent. When we hit the deck, I want every warrior to storm off the Pod wearing your war face and carrying your railguns as if ready for a battle. Then transition into formation. Lock your bodies at the position of attention and prepare to march. Let the intimidation begin. We are already earning Flayse credits, so let's put on a good show, right up to the point that we take charge."

The warriors on board the shuttles shouted hearty "oorahs" and settled in for the rest of the descent. Christina's anxiety started to rise, creating a lump in her throat. She'd just bet the entire Bad Company on their ability to flex to the unknown. The number of variables seemed to grow as the ground approached. She closed her eyes and took a deep breath. Then another.

"Thirty seconds to debarkation," Smedley noted.

Christina opened her eyes and stood up. She looked from face to face. Fierce. Warriors. Ready for action.

The drop ship touched down without a sound and the ramp descended.

"GO!" Christina started the exodus, running to her position on the parade ground. She scanned the bleachers on both sides, looking to fill in her gaps in knowledge. A mech pounded past her, and the audience gasped.

She found it oddly calming. *Smedley, start scanning faces. I need to know who's here and who's not right fucking now.*

The AI was already collecting and collating data from the Pods' external sensors, but he added the stream of information coming from the mechs.

Entering the parade ground as if they were conducting an attack had sent the Flayse handlers running for cover. The area was clear of interlopers or innocent bystanders, whichever they were. The mechs held them at bay.

It seemed like forever before the Bad Company was in formation and still. In reality, it had taken less than a minute for all six drop ships to disgorge their passengers and dust off, hovering where they could be quickly recalled without being in immediate danger from an attack.

The Bad Company stood alone in the kill zone—afraid, yet their courage, honor, and commitment kept them from showing it. Their professionalism as warriors had each running through emergency combat actions in their minds. They were ready to act while the trepidation of waiting for an attack weighed on their souls.

Black Eagles, make your pass, Christina ordered.

The two space fighters screamed into the zone, before coming to a near-stop over the parade field. They crossed in front of the stands at a snail's pace before standing on their tails and rocketing into the sky. More oohs and aahs from the crowd. Christina kept her eyes on the Magnate. She was able to pick him out of the crowd.

Joseph and Petricia were nodding and glad-handing their way past the front row. Cory and Dokken hovered near the Flayse, standing out as they tried to look inconspicuous. There were no other animals of any sort in the area. Dokken didn't care. He looked around before raising his leg and marking a corner post marking off the bleacher area.

The Magnate of the Flayse Conglomeration and the Chairman of the Frikandan Cooperative are both here, along with their top ten subordinates.

That complicates things, Christina replied, eyes darting across the broad area, looking for the threat she knew was there. The one that Joseph couldn't confirm and the VIPs seemed oblivious to.

CHAPTER EIGHTEEN

Band Rayal Seven, Okkoto

Tonie and Terry lumbered through the corridor, supporting each other until Terry healed sufficiently to walk by himself, but Tonie was still dogged.

"Not much farther," Tonie said softly, not looking up from the floor. Terry massaged the pouch with the remainder of his water, knowing that it wasn't enough for both of them.

He handed it to Tonie. "Drink."

They stopped so the Erthos could down the last bit.

"We need to find a place to refill that."

"I think there's a rest facility next to the control room. It's not much farther," Tonie repeated. They began walking again, and Terry crouched to let Tonie rest his arm over his shoulder.

"How much time do we have left?" Terry asked.

Tonie grimaced but didn't answer.

"That much, huh?" Terry expected that it would be any

moment now that the power would turn back on. That the Etheric force field would rage into place and renew its attack on Char, if it had ever subsided. Terry half-picked up the Erthos and propelled them both forward.

Tonie hung on, pointing ahead until he stabbed his finger at the last doorway. Terry removed both laser pistols and stood ready.

"You won't need those," Tonie said and activated the door. Terry raised the weapons and followed the Erthos in as if breaching an enemy stronghold. The room was filled with equipment, and it was significantly larger than the room where Terry had found the engineer.

"Why don't you work in here?" Terry asked. He stuffed the laser pistols into his pockets. Without filled water flasks, there was room. Water or weapons—it wasn't a hard choice. "Looks to have a lot more going on in here."

"Sometimes I do, but the other control room is the master over the power systems. This is everything that operates using the Etheric energy. Here are the hydroponic controls." He waved at a heavy equipment tower with a small access screen. "Environmental controls. Cleaning systems. Food processing. Waste management. Resource extraction..." He continued with a long list of everything needed to keep the outpost functional and its people alive.

Terry waved impatiently. "Maybe some other time. Send the elevator down and have it waiting for us, ready to return to the surface."

"Yes. That would be over here." Tonie worked his way into a far corner, and Terry followed him. Everything seemed to be running, even though the corridor lights were still off. "Have the generators kicked back on?"

Tonie held his tongue and nodded tersely.

"How long?" Terry demanded. He started to shake his leg and rock back and forth. "Forget it. Hurry!"

The Erthos started tapping buttons. "I have to reprogram a couple of things. Hang on. Next door is a rest facility. Maybe get some water?"

"Wristband." Terry held out his hand. He had tossed his security bot summoning device and needed one that worked if he wanted back in. Tonie handed it over without complaint.

Terry hurried out. When the door opened, the lights in the corridor were on. His hand started to shake with the pressure of his impending failure. *Hang on, Char,* he said. He tried to use his comm chip, but the dampening field that hid the complex also disabled their internal communication.

Flayse Conglomerate, Efluyez Homeworld, Alganor Sector

First Platoon, designated target is the Magnate and his senior leadership. There are ten that we need. Smedley, transmit the images to their helmets. Second Platoon, you have the Flayse. First ten get saved, the rest are on their own. It'll be a tight squeeze on the drop ships, but jam them in there. We aren't leaving any of ours behind. Christina looked left and right.

The unit was formed, and the crowd had silenced. The Black Eagles were nowhere to be seen. The Magnate seemed to wear a perpetual scowl. Maybe the mechs rubbed him the wrong way. Maybe his seat was uncomfortable. One never knew the discord prevalent in a totalitarian's life.

The waiting was over. It was time. She turned the formation to the right and gave the order. "Forward, March!" As one they stepped forward, cloaks swishing in rhythm except for the four-legged platoon. They held their cloaks tightly shut to keep from exposing the heavy weapons they carried underneath.

Anything? Christina asked.

The mechs report no unusual activity, Smedley relayed.

Nothing to report here either, except that the Magnate is quite impressed with how the Bad Company has presented itself, Joseph said.

"I'll be damned," Christina said to herself. She didn't need to call cadence. The four mechs pounded the ground in unison, delivering the beat to which the Bad Company marched.

The formation turned left at a post marking the corner. To get the ranks lined up afterward, the outer personnel extended their strides while those on the inner corner shortened theirs, stepping to a standard eighty-centimeter stride length once they were back on track. All of that took only five paces before the formation was back as a single entity headed in the same direction.

Christina had to force herself to breathe. She was as tight as a piano wire, unable to relax with the anticipation. Kimber marched with the four-legged platoon, the three warriors at the back of the formation with mechs hammering the ground with a steady beat.

The first rank approached the Magnate. Joseph gave the

signal, and they snapped their railguns from their shoulders to a two-handed carry in front of their chests, the standard port arms position.

Colonel Terry Henry Walton had determined early in the conflict-resolution enterprise's existence that the warriors would never salute another power. They saluted within their own chain of command and the colonel saluted foreign dignitaries, but only for a reason, not from custom. When the unit passed the VIPs, they did so combat ready.

That didn't matter. Joseph raised his hand in alarm, but it was too late. The ground erupted beneath the Bad Company in a massive and violent explosion. Warriors were thrown.

One mech started to fire its oversized railgun before a second one joined the cacophony of chaos.

Band Rayal Seven, Okkoto

Terry splashed his face and tasted the water before refilling his one pouch. He returned to the control room, expecting a fight or something strange in the five paces between the two rooms, but nothing happened.

Inside, Tonie worked diligently to deliver the elevator as a way out of the Erthos shelter. He frowned, tapped buttons, swiped his fingers across the screen, tapped more, and kept frowning.

Terry had had enough. "I have to go check on Char. We'll meet you at the elevator. Do or die, my man. It's now or never." Clichés were the only thing that came to mind, but Tonie had probably never heard them. Terry rushed from the room without returning Tonie's wristband.

Terry needed it more than he did.

TH ran down the corridor, trying to get his bearings. It wasn't long before he was lost. He tried a number of doors, but they didn't tell him where he was or how to get where he wanted to go.

He retraced his steps to the control room. When he entered, Tonie was gone.

Terry leaned back into the corridor and bellowed the Erthos' name. "Tonie!" He ran in the general direction of where he thought he needed to go, yelling down every corridor, listening, and moving on. After fifteen minutes, he began to realize how big the complex was. They had entered and explored only one small corner of it.

Once again, Terry retraced his steps. "Every left. Keep taking lefts," he told himself out loud. He started to run as fast as he could, hitting dead ends and backtracking.

He heard the sound before he saw it, but he didn't have time to mess with it. The hovering security bot appeared around a corner just as he reached it. He pinned it against the wall with a forearm, despite the screaming pain from where it tried to burn his arm with its forcefield, but that didn't last long. Terry shoved his pistol up from below and fired, letting the laser burn into it. Once he had a hole, he twisted the pistol to scramble the bot's mechanical guts.

It died without a spark or flash. He let it drop to the floor and returned to running.

"Tonie!" he shouted as he did in each corridor. This time there was a response. "Tonie?"

The Erthos stepped into an intersection and waved for Terry.

"You acted like you knew where you were going."

"I didn't," Terry admitted. Around the corner, TH's face fell when he saw the immensity of the rock fall.

"It's not that bad," Tonie said, trying to restore hope to the crushed man. "We only need to get right there!" He stabbed a finger at a point on the edge of the fall. Terry could see the corner and the empty space of a corridor beyond.

"What are we waiting for?" Terry clambered up the rubble and ripped at the stones with his bare hands. His left arm kept betraying him as the nanocytes struggled against the damage and the new demands being made of it, but the force of Terry's will kept him churning through the debris until he made a hole big enough to crawl through.

He wiggled into it and slid head-first down the fall that spread into the dining room corridor.

"Go on," Tonie said, waving as he took more care pushing himself through the opening.

Terry ran the short distance to the dining room. When the door opened, he saw Char holding her head and moaning. BA sat next to her, looking as if she were lost in thought.

Bethany Anne slowly opened her eyes. "It's about fucking time. What were you doing, clipping your toenails? Getting a massage? Taking a power nap?" BA looked rather annoyed.

"How is she?" Terry asked, dodging past the Queen on his way to embrace Char.

"*She* has been better," Char mumbled.

"We're close. Tonie has called the elevator." Terry kissed the top of Char's head and held her tight.

"Tonie has put everything in place so that he can call the elevator," Tonie called in a tired voice from the doorway. He was dirty from crawling through the rock fall.

"Don't mess with me, Tonie." Terry stood before lifting Char into his arms. "We're leaving. Right now."

"I have to do some work in the elevator control room first, but come on. It's right around the corner." Tonie gestured for his wristband, but Terry's hands were underneath Char.

"We'll figure it out when we get there." Terry nodded to Bethany Anne.

"You finally are able to execute your plan. Bravo, TH. Have your people call my people, and we'll do lunch."

"Of course, BA. You need to visit Keeg Station." He adjusted his hold on Char so her head missed a wall. "We'll ply you with Moonstokle Pie until you beat all of us senseless."

Bethany Anne followed them into the corridor. "I have to ask, yet I'm already regretting my actions. What are you talking about?"

"Moonstokle looks and tastes like pineapple..."

BA's mouth dropped open. "Stop right there, you dripping nipple-twunt."

"Can't stop. Saving Char's life," Terry said over his shoulder as he hurried after Tonie. BA raced ahead.

"It's illegal as fuck to put pineapple on pizza!" BA wasn't joking.

"It's not pineapple," he argued back.

"Don't mince words with me."

"Your lawyer loves it. Rivka is a huge fan. A gentleman by the name of Frankfurter once said, 'All our work, our whole life, is a matter of semantics because words are the tools with which we work, the material out of which laws are made, out of which the Constitution was written. Everything depends on our understanding of them.'"

"You're quoting a wiener? Is that like talking out your ass but facing the other way?" BA loped alongside Terry while Tonie shuffled ahead, pointing left at the last door before the short hallway to the elevator. "Are you saying I don't understand words?"

"I'm saying that maybe you don't know a good pizza when it's placed before you."

"That's it, TH. You are off my Christmas card list."

Terry leaned close with Char still in his arms until his wristband activated the door. Tonie pushed through while the door was still sliding to the side. The room was little more than a closet with a panel attached to the wall.

Terry nuzzled Char's head, but she was out cold. He let his face hover close to her nose to make sure she was still breathing. "My every breath is yours," he told her.

Bethany Anne watched carefully, eyes shifting between the werewolf and the Erthos engineer.

"*Faster, motherfucker,*" she growled.

Tonie ignored her. He had quickly developed the talent after spending time with Terry Henry. Arcs sparked from the box, and Tonie cheered. The elevator doors opened, then closed and opened again.

Terry approached the elevator carefully. The doors finally stayed open long enough for him to ease his way inside, Char still in his arms. "Are you two coming?" he asked.

Tonie hopped from the room and started running but stopped when he saw the door was stuck.

"This is a problem."

Char's breaths were coming too slowly, and her skin was starting to turn blue. Terry jammed his eyes closed and prayed for a miracle.

CHAPTER NINETEEN

<u>**Flayse Conglomerate, Efluyez Homeworld, Alganor Sector**</u>

"Scatter!" Christina ordered. She'd kept her feet through the blast that had ripped from beneath the turf upon which they'd all been standing. The cloaks had provided some protection, and the helmets had let them retain their heads and their wits. A concussion blast, no shrapnel. Unprotected troops would have suffered crushing injuries.

Those directly above the explosives never knew what hit them. The blast came from below, directing the force into their bodies and using their cloaks as funnels until the cloaks were ripped away.

Bodies lined the parade deck, but the rest were already running. The crowd was screaming, and those in the front rows were shoved into those behind. Braced against the bleacher supports, they were crushed. The Magnate was in a separate box, protected independently. He stood with bleeding ears. Joseph and Petricia picked their way through the injured as they climbed to get to the Magnate and the VIPs surrounding him.

On the other side of the field, Cory picked herself up, uninjured because of the cloak's protection.

That sucked, Dokken complained before collecting his wits. *There are injured.*

As warriors ran past her to secure the Frikandan Chairman and his entourage, Cory ran the other way into the settling dust of the landmines.

The mechs stopped firing.

What were you firing at? Do we have targets? Christina asked.

Not anymore, we don't. Seconds before the explosion, we detected two vehicles detach from the parking area and accelerate in this direction, Cap explained.

Christina found his logic sound.

Joseph?

Magnate is secured. Joseph had wrapped his boat cloak over the leader of the Flayse Conglomerate, and he waved from the stands as the Bad Company warriors spread out in an arc surrounding the Magnate and his people.

The mechs took positions on the four corners of the mangled parade deck. The four-legged platoon had been thrown about but was out of the primary blast area.

Two Black Eagles appeared and made tight spirals as they circled the area, ready to fire on anything that moved in a way they didn't like.

Weapons tight, Christina ordered. *Joseph?*

Not anyone over here, he told her as if he knew her question. *Recover to the parade deck and let's get the hell out of here.*

Cory rushed past Christina to care for the warriors mixed in with the craters and uprooted turf. The first two she found were alive but badly injured. Not bleeding, but the crushing blows had done serious damage to their insides.

Summon the cryo-drones, Cory ordered. A single drone had been strapped to the outside of each Pod. Smedley turned them loose, and they proceeded under their own power to the ambush site. *I need some help.*

Four-legged platoon, at your service, Bundin replied, running amazingly quickly on his stumpy legs. The Yollin and the Ixtali outpaced him, arriving first to provide helping hands to lift the injured into the drones.

As the trio took charge of the first pair, Cory moved on to a warrior, crushed to death from the power of the explosion. "Must have been standing right on top of it," Cory lamented as she used his cloak to keep him together to lift and put him into a cryo-drone. She activated the controls and froze him, giving the man a chance at being saved.

Dokken ran ahead, barking to identify where he found the injured. Five more—too many for the drones.

They all needed help. She leaned over the worst of the survivors and held her hands to his chest, but his injuries were too deep. She ordered him into a drone, and the four-legged platoon took care of him. The next was the same. And the next.

No more drones, and two who might die. Cory placed her hands on them and willed her nanocytes to work their magic, but she couldn't feel the injuries. They were too deep, and her nanos had to stay close to her hands so she could feed them Etheric energy.

More warriors showed up to help as the two delegations stared daggers at each other under the watchful eye of the Bad Company. The drop ships appeared and hovered, looking for clear space to land. They moved to the side of the parade deck.

That wasn't good enough for Cory.

Get a Pod here NOW! We need to get these warriors back to the War Axe. *No one dies today. Do you hear me? No one dies!*

Band Rayal Seven, Okkoto

Tonie hung his head in a combination of exhaustion and failure.

"What's wrong with it?" BA stormed into the room and looked at the panel.

"Energy's not flowing through it right or something. It's bungled."

Her eyes traveled around the panel, searching for anything to give her a clue. "Not on my watch," Bethany Anne said softly.

She moved to where he could see her, closed her eyes, and held her hands up. Etheric power arced around her body, dancing off the walls and through the panel. Terry backed up with Char in his arms and continued until he was on the elevator. Tonie was torn between staying at the panel and counting on the strange being to complete the circuit.

He chose the elevator. "I guess I'm coming with you."

Terry nodded, hoping his willpower kept Char alive

until they could get out from under the crush of Etheric energy.

BA opened her eyes long enough to wink at TH. *"Move!"* She mouthed.

The doors slammed shut, and the elevator started to rise.

Flayse Conglomerate, Efluyez Homeworld, Alganor Sector

The cryo-drones secured themselves to the roofs of the Pods while the warriors boarded. The mechs were the farthest away, so they had to wait for them to board while cattle-herding the VIPs onto the two drop ships that wouldn't be carrying the armor.

Slikira ran back along the parade route to pick up dropped weapons. She had lost one of the mortars and was concerned that it could fall into the wrong hands. She found two railguns and a warrior's cloak. The Ixtali were extremely fast, and she made up for her delay by running at full speed into a Pod.

Cory nurtured the wounded while pumping her fist for the group to hurry. "Button us up and take us home," Christina ordered, finding herself on the same ship as Cory. *Kimber, you're the last one out.*

I'll make sure we don't leave anyone behind, the major reported, sending two warriors over the parade deck for one last scrub before her Pod departed. The Magnate was less than amused at being abducted from his own planet.

After Kimber had boarded and signaled for the ship to

take off, the Magnate squeezed through the mass of bodies to stand toe to toe with the major.

"Can I help you, Magnate?"

"I demand to be taken to my palace."

"I am in no position to grant your request. Warrior. Following orders. Your regime is under threat, and we are ensuring your safety. That is what people hire us for."

"I assure you that I will be safe in my own palace."

"I would have thought you could ensure the safety of your guests, but that assumption was wrong, so we'll stop making assumptions. We'll do what we know is right. You and your people, as well as the Frikandans, are being taken to the *War Axe*, neutral ground, where you two will work out an agreement before you can return to Efluyez."

"There is no need for such a stunt. We already had an agreement. Couldn't you see that they were on the same field as we were? That their lives were threatened, just like ours?"

"What I see is that you seem indifferent to the fact that someone attacked us. If we lost any warriors today, you are going to pay."

"We're already paying. Half a million credits! Take the loss out of that," the Magnate retorted.

Kimber cooled to the point of freezing, and the other warriors backed away as much as they could within the confined space of the drop ship. "Why were we attacked?"

"What?" the Magnate shot back dismissively with a half-shrug.

"We were attacked while under your protection. Since you've abrogated your responsibility, we have no problem picking up the slack, as it may be. Your failure has resulted in the Bad Company taking over. Your half-million credits are nothing compared to what you're going to end up paying when this is over." Kimber's tone was low and steady.

Dangerous.

The Magnate caught the magnitude of her words. "You can't. The Federation doesn't interfere in the internal politics of signatory worlds!"

Kimber pointed at her people, who were pressing in on the Magnate and his delegation. The warriors loomed over the shorter Flayse. One of the VIPs grabbed at a railgun, earning himself a punch in the face. He had no chance of taking the weapon.

"Looks like we can and we have," Kimber continued, tipping her chin at the warrior who had resisted the attack.

"I will call Reynolds!" the Magnate blustered.

"Fuck off," Kimber told him. Her hand vibrated with the desire to grab the Magnate by the throat, but someone had to be the adult. "Here's what's going to happen. We're going to put you and the Frikandans in a room together, and you are going to hammer out a non-aggression and mutual-trade pact. During your negotiations, you're going to come clean on who planned the attack on us. Then the Bad Company is going to take those people into custody and give them a fair trial. If they are found guilty, they'll go to the prison planet of Jiordaan."

"Fair trial. From the Federation? Is that what I've just gotten? I've been kidnapped!"

"Tell it to the Magistrate. I'm sure she'll be delighted to hear your take on things. And let me tell you, if any of my people die, you'll be right there with the terrorists in Jiordaan, serving your time, side by side with your fellow criminals. You failed us. You failed your people. And *that* is why we are now in charge. Shut your mouth before I put my fist in it."

One of the Flayse put his hand on the Magnate's shoulder and whispered something into his ear. Kimber heard it and smiled as the Magnate harrumphed and turned his back on her.

Please stop pissing her off. They have guns!

<hr>

Cory attended to the wounded as well as she could. Water. Pain medication. The Bad Company had been boosted, getting treatments from the Pod-doc, but limited in case anyone left. Their nanos would fail over time. They could heal injuries unless the damage was too great. The warriors were borderline.

Christina urged the drop ship to greater speed, but it was already topped out. Smedley was bringing them home as fast as possible. The *War Axe* had moved into a lower orbit to shorten the distance.

Still, it was taking time.

One of the warriors started to spasm. They'd all seen it before. Death throes.

"We're coming in hot," Christina told the *War Axe*. "We have one for immediate transfer to the Pod-doc."

The Pod didn't slow down until right before it passed through the forcefield at the entrance to the heavy destroyer's hangar bay. The warrior sighed his last breath with the buffeting of a radical maneuver to place the ramp close to the mobile Pod-doc units at the back of the hangar bay. The Bad Company had developed them because too many times they'd raced back to the *War Axe* exactly like this, carrying the injured. The cryo-drones were one piece of the battle-wounded puzzle. Instant access to a Pod-doc was another, without exposing the technology to a potential enemy.

The ramp dropped, and two warriors grabbed the injured and ran, Cory and Dokken right behind them. They waited while Cory manually activated the Pod-doc. The hatch popped, she lifted it, and they put the man inside. "Smedley, this thing better be working."

Once the hatch had closed and secured, Smedley took over.

"We have all eight nominally operational, but some of the automated controls will have to come later. And the injured may require further treatments in our primary system. These are limited to main procedures at present." He hadn't told Cory anything she didn't know. Maybe he was reiterating it for those in the area who were concerned for their teammates.

It was about morale. It was easier to convince a warrior to take risks if he knew that his unit would do everything possible to save him should he be injured. That was already the case, but they were bringing more technology to bear.

The galaxy was a dangerous place.

Two other warriors had picked up the other injured man, using his cloak as an ad-hoc stretcher. They waited at the next mobile Pod-doc for Cory to start the system. After a few deft touches, the lid popped and they place him inside. She turned Smedley loose on the second treatment.

"We have six more coming, Smedley. They are in cryo, so there isn't the rush. One already flatlined, so he's first. We got him into stasis within a couple of minutes. I hope that was quick enough."

"Know that I will do all that I can, as you have done, Cordelia," the AI reassured her. Dokken rubbed against her leg. She wasn't as exhausted as if she'd used her nanocytes to treat the injured—not that she hadn't tried.

"Take it easy," Christina said softly. "You've done all that could be done and put our good people into the right hands. Thank you."

Christina one-arm-hugged her friend.

"No one is going to die today," Cory whispered.

"Not today," Christina agreed. "Close, but no cigar. We shall party well once we get these cockwads straightened out." Christina's expression hardened. "Speak of the devil."

The other Pods landed with less aggressive maneuvering than what Smedley had done for Christina's drop ship.

"Get those cryo-drones down here and in line!" Christina ordered, never taking her eyes off the newly arrived Pods. She waited for the ramps to drop and them to disgorge their passengers.

"Keep our guests separated."

After the last drop ship had landed, Kai raced into the bay with a team to move tables and chairs to a spot close to the open door where space would provide the backdrop for the negotiations. This part of Christina's plan had been a contingency just in case, but Kai played his role well, even though he'd only had a few hours to get everything ready.

Jenelope appeared, with Xianna and two maintenance bots acting as food carriers. They decorated the tables and set out a small tray of local snacks while avoiding looking at the wounded. Xianna sighed in relief when she saw her husband, but then felt guilty about it. He pointed to the injured and gave her the thumbs up. "We're okay," he mouthed.

The drop ships had emptied. The Black Eagles had parked near the portable Pod-docs, with Aaron and Yanmei joining Cory to stand by and wait for good news.

The Frikandans were led to one side of the massive hangar bay, and the Flayse to the other. The two delegations stood apart, silently watching each other.

Christina took a deep breath and walked into the area between them, then waved for them to come closer. Cap and Kelly in their mechs moved with them, staying nearby.

Intimidation—something the Bad Company was getting better at with each operation. Joseph stood nearby, helmet cradled in the crook of his arm. Petricia was by his side, her helmet nowhere to be seen.

"I don't know which of you attacked us—" Christina didn't finish before the outburst.

"Not us!" they cried together. "It was..." They both declared the other side to be the culprit, the terrorist.

Joseph turned toward the Frikandan delegation and pointed to the second to last person in line. Petricia walked over and yanked that person out of line.

"What are you doing with my finance minister?" the chairman demanded.

Petricia dragged him closer to Joseph. "Outrageous!" the minister shouted. "Get your claws off me."

Joseph moved forward and leaned close until their foreheads were nearly touching. He tried to push the vampire away, but Petricia caught his arms from behind and locked them next to his soft body.

He'd spent too much time making backroom deals to remain fit.

"Why did you do this?" Joseph looked into his mind to find the answers.

"I didn't!" The minister's denials were growing weaker.

Joseph turned to look at the Flayse. He didn't see the face from the finance minister's mind. "Do you have a city planning commissioner?"

The Magnate's jaw dropped. "I *knew* he was angling to undermine me!" He turned to face one of those with him. "Have him arrested immediately."

The other Flayse held their hands up in surrender, powerless to comply with the order.

Joseph nodded at Christina, and she motioned for two warriors to seize the finance minister. "Put him in the brig. Joseph, if you would be so kind as to share what you learned?"

"After we take our seats and get a drink." Joseph pointed to the tables and smiled. "You are much closer to a resolution than you realize."

CHAPTER TWENTY

Band Rayal Seven, Okkoto

Char wasn't improving. Terry had hoped the effect would be immediate, but it wasn't.

"I don't know what else to do," Terry said.

"There *is* nothing else to do," Tonie replied.

The elevator continued to rise. The Erthos' eyes shot wide in shock right before he disintegrated, becoming nothing more than dust particles filling the elevator. Terry covered his mouth as Char took a deep breath, her chest heaving with the effort.

"Cover your mouth," he cautioned as he put a sleeve over her face. She continued to take deep but quick breaths until she opened her eyes.

The air cleared in the elevator as it continued to rise.

"Where..." Char couldn't finish her question.

"Finally on our way back to the surface." Terry set her on her unsteady feet. "We've escaped the outpost."

"Finally," Char confirmed. She looked at the empty elevator. "Where's Bethany Anne?"

"She saved us by using herself to power the elevator. Tonie couldn't finish it, and then the doors closed. That was the last I saw of her, and Tonie dissolved when we passed through the Etheric shield. I guess there was more to the clones than just meat and bones."

"How are you feeling?" Terry asked. It was the best he could come up with. He didn't want to tell her she looked like she'd spent too much time on death's doorstep, so he settled on an alternative. "You are so beautiful."

"I look like shit," she replied.

"At least it wasn't me who said it." Terry chuckled.

"But you're thinking it," Char mumbled, still trying to gather herself as her nanocytes struggled for normalcy. Her sensitivity to the Etheric had made her vulnerable to the Etheric power coursing beneath the Okkoto moon. She needed time.

"You are so beautiful," Terry said again.

"And you are such a *man*."

"Guilty. Time to get the fuck off this rock and back to our vacation."

"I think I'd rather just go home."

"We can do that too," Terry agreed. "We will do whatever you want."

The elevator stopped, and Terry craned his neck to look through the access hatch in the roof. "It's dark up there." He interlaced his fingers and held them down for Char to step into. He hoisted her up, and she struggled to pull herself through.

Terry crouched and vaulted as high as he could, barely high enough to get his fingertips on the ledge. He did a pull-up until he could get his elbow over, then crawled out to find himself where they'd started however long ago. Their rope was still hanging from above.

Char grabbed it tightly and started climbing, walking up the side of the shaft. Terry held the bottom of the rope out, keeping tension on it to make it easier. The elevator shifted beneath his feet and then started to drop, and he clung to the rope as if his life depended on it. Char almost lost her grip, freezing in place to make sure she didn't fall.

Terry let go with one hand and braced himself to catch his wife, but no one fell and time crawled. Slowly, Terry took the rope in two hands.

"I'll be there in a minute," he said as calmly as he could manage. He figured he could survive the fall, even all five hundred feet, but Char wouldn't, not after returning to the other side of the Etheric shield.

"I'm fine. Heading for the top now." She saved her breath and soon was over the top, with Terry right behind her. He found her lying on her back, spread-eagled like a sacrifice to the gods. "It's nice being outside, even though it's a bit frigid."

"I'll second that. Maybe we can still get in a few vacation days in the sun, enjoy nothing more than being outside."

"Maybe." Char closed her eyes and concentrated on breathing. Clouds appeared before her face with each effort.

Terry removed the communication device from his pocket and activated it. "Venus, this is Terry Henry Walton requesting immediate pick up from Okkoto, over."

Unlike when he had tested it when the shuttle was on

Okkoto, there was no response of any kind. Terry didn't think it was transmitting.

It was cold outside, just like they said it would be. It had been cold in the daylight, but in the darkness, it was already pressing in on them.

Terry kept trying, lying next to Char to share their body heat, but the ground was sucking it away more than the air. "We have to find shelter," Terry said. Char grimaced as if he'd stabbed her.

"I know. This is our life, TH. We go from one death-defying crisis to the next," she mumbled.

Terry helped her stand, supporting her once she was upright. "But we always survive. *Always.*"

He hoped that the shuttle would return with the daylight, whenever that would be. They had one flask of water and one protein bar between them. He knew that hope was no replacement for a good plan.

The *War Axe*, in orbit around the Efluyez Homeworld, Alganor Sector

Christina stabbed her fingernails into her palms for the fourth time in the last minute. The delegates continued to argue despite the triviality of their points. She had no patience for stupid. She wanted to give the warriors her attention, but Kimber was there, guiding the efforts to get the injured into the Pod-docs, clean the weapons and their gear, and return to combat readiness as quickly as possible before standing down.

Joseph was losing patience too, but his telepathy gave

him an edge. He knew what they were thinking, and it was time for the players to put their cards on the table.

He walked into the middle area between the tables and held his hands up for silence. Both sides kept talking, neither listening to the other.

"Silence!" he shouted, fixing the Magnate with a glare before turning and giving the same look to the chairman. "The time for games is over. Your people worked together to plot a coup against you both. Maybe you should think about how unhappy your own people are. Here is what's going on in your minds."

Joseph walked to the member of the Frikandan delegation who sat on the far end. "You want to work your way up and will say whatever you think they want to hear. Half of you have that same attitude, but deep down," Joseph stooped to look the VIP in the eye, "you want what is best for your people.

"You all need to understand that the only power you have is granted by your citizens. You are both so-called passive societies, but you are violent, arrogant, and extremely aggressive. Maybe that's because no one knees you in the groin when you deserve it. I don't know, but you and you..." Joseph pointed to the Magnate and the chairman and motioned for them to stand.

They hesitated long enough to express their displeasure at being ordered about, but not so long as to get knees to their privates.

"You both want education, trade, peace, and power. Guess what you'll have if you implement trade agreements that bring prosperity? All the power you ever wanted to do right by your people. You already live in palaces, so what else could you possibly want? Now listen closely." Joseph looked from one to the other. "They will never worship you. The Kurtherians tried that bullshit. Guess who is being hunted throughout the universe and destroyed when they are found? Being a god isn't what you expect.

"And we don't tolerate false gods in the Federation. I can see in your minds that isn't what you want, but you both want more power. More. More. More!" Joseph approached the Magnate and slammed his hand on the table.

"That stops here!" Joseph growled. His vampire fangs appeared, and he relaxed. He had no intention of biting anyone. He didn't crave blood, but he was angry and tired. The Bad Company had driven hard to be ready for something so simple yet complex as a parade.

"As part of your negotiation, the Federation is going to insert a clause that should you oppress your people or each other, you will be forcibly removed from power. Period."

"You can't," the Magnate stated, lifting his chin and frowning. "It's too subjective."

Joseph smiled. His teeth were still elongated, and the Magnate couldn't take his eyes from them. "Yes, it is. If you want us to come back here, take unto yourselves power for power's sake. Your war of words and thoughts is over. You will work out your treaty. You have four hours to draft a document. We will leave you to it. If you have nothing when we return, we'll tell you what you're going to do because we'll be the ones enforcing it." Joseph waited through the angry looks before adding, "Smedley, target both of our august leaders' palaces. Prepare to fire."

The chairman raised his hand and yelled, "*NO!* My family's in there."

"So there *is* something you care about more than yourself?" Joseph looked at the chairman's resigned expression. He nodded.

"We'll leave you to it." Joseph strolled away, taking Petricia's hand as they sauntered across the hangar bay.

"If you'll excuse me, I have things I need to attend to." Christina smiled at the delegations because she was happy to be leaving them. "I look forward to the celebration of your new treaty."

She made a beeline for the Pod-docs.

"Can you believe they would do that?" the Magnate asked looking at his Frikandan counterpart.

"You hired violent people to do exactly what they are doing—use force and intimidation. But *they* are dictating the end result, not you, and that is where you underestimated them. That is where we both underestimated the Federation. Please, let us talk like adults, and you..." the chairman fixed his delegation with a steely gaze, "tell me what you think, not what you think I want to hear."

***

Kai had produced a couple of chairs and was sitting on one, with Cory sitting on the other. She was slumped against him where he held her tightly.

"Sleeping," he mouthed to Christina.

She pointed to the Pod-docs and gave a thumbs-up with a hopeful look.

He nodded and smiled.

Smedley, status of my people? she asked.

Alive and recovering. We have three more from cryo to get into the Pod-docs, but we'll put them through the primary equipment in sickbay when it is ready.

Thank you, Smedley. It's nice to get good news. Terry may not be happy about the whole thing, but in the end, I think we've made a difference for the average citizen of the Federation. I do think TH will like those boat cloaks and helmets though, Christina added. Now free of the burden of Bad Company deaths when she was left in charge, her thoughts cascaded out of her in a stream of consciousness. *Why do we call it sickbay? No one is sick, and it's not a bay. Have you been in touch with TH? No, don't. I'll deliver the report, at least as much as we have right now. How is my dad doing? Did we ever learn where that invisible destroyer came from?*

We call it sickbay because that's what Colonel Walton calls it, a holdover from his days in the Marine Corps. We have not heard from him or Charumati at all but aren't they supposed to be on vacation? I think Mister Lowell is doing well. Why don't you call him? He and your mother enjoy hearing from you. There was no signature that we could backtrack. Looking for a race that can make themselves invisible is as problematic as it sounds. We don't even know where to start our search. I think I've answered all your questions.

You're an AI, so you know you've answered the questions I posed. No one has heard from Terry and Char? I'm heading to my quarters now. Spool up the comm system, I'm making a call.

The comm system is active. You could call right now if you wish, Smedley offered.

Let me have my moment. I'm old-school. I like talking out loud when making a call.

CHAPTER TWENTY-ONE

The _War Axe_, in orbit around the Efluyez Homeworld, Alganor Sector

"We are very concerned," the voice replied from the resort on the Venus moon. "They were not waiting when the shuttle returned for them. They have not contacted us, and we have been unable to ping their communication device. We fear the worst."

"What did your search party find?"

"We didn't send a search party. We are monitoring the channel, waiting for them to contact us."

"Why didn't you send a search party?" Christina avoided going on an expletive-laden tirade.

"They took an expedition to another moon. We cannot be responsible for anything not on our property. We are not equipped for off-moon search and recovery. We have notified the authorities on Cygnus VI, but they signed a waiver. They understood all this. I will transmit a copy of their waiver and contract upon verification of your credentials."

"Of course they signed a waiver." Christina pinched the bridge of her nose. She could feel her blood pressure rising. "Thank you."

She tapped her screen. "Smedley, get me the authorities on Cygnus VI."

When she was connected, she received the same runaround. She disconnected while they were still explaining how they'd done everything they could with a single pass of Okkoto.

"Micky, we need to go to the Venus Pleasure Moon right now."

"I didn't know you thought about me like that, but what about Kai?" Micky joked.

"No one has heard from Terry and Char."

"We can be there in ten minutes," Micky replied, and the connection went dead.

Christina ran from her quarters, headed down the corridor, and hit the stairs at a sprint. She jumped from one landing to the next until she was on the hangar deck level. She raced toward the delegation, where a congenial conversation was taking place.

"Listen up," she shouted. "You've got three minutes to seal the deal and board the Pod. We have to go, and I have no idea when we could get back. I can spare one drop ship to take you home. Thank you for your time. Keep us apprised of your negotiations. We will return to enforce the treaty."

No one moved.

"What are you waiting for?" She stepped aside and motioned toward the Pod.

One of the VIPs pointed at her. She looked down to see that she was only in her underwear.

She stood up straight. "So what? Board the Pod, because you don't want to go where we're going."

They moved with surprising speed for a bunch of out-of-shape aliens.

"Where are you going?" one of them asked as he passed.

She thought for a moment. The Venus Pleasure Moon. Maybe they didn't need to know that part. "Classified."

As soon as the Pod cleared the forcefield and took a sharp turn toward the planet, a Gate formed before the *War Axe.*

Kai materialized and wrapped a boat cloak around Christina's shoulders.

"I guess I better get dressed," she said with a soft smile.

"It *is* a pleasure moon." Kai's heart wasn't in the jest. "Where are they?"

"We will find out. We're not leaving without them, even if we have to find and board every ship that's been through here to make sure they didn't leave against their will."

"What if they disappeared as part of a master plan to pass the torch to the next generation?" Kai wondered.

Christina thought about it for a moment. "Bullshit. That's not Terry Henry Walton. He would retire to his bar first. It's almost rebuilt, and there's no way he'd leave without making sure it's producing quality beer once again."

"Beer?" Kai didn't follow her logic, but he accepted the result. No, Terry Henry was hopelessly honest. He wouldn't disappear like that.

· · ·

Venus Pleasure Moon, Cygnus VI

Smedley maneuvered the drop ship with Christina, Kai, Joseph, Petricia, Cory, Dokken, Kimber, and Auburn out of the hangar bay and into space. It was a short descent through the atmosphere to the Venus resort. None of them were in a party mood as they sought answers regarding the disappearance of their family and friends.

"You didn't all need to come," Christina said. They smirked or returned blank looks. They had no choice because it was what Terry and Char would have done for them. "But I'm glad you're here."

"We'll get to the bottom of it," Cory assured her.

"Occam's razor," Joseph suggested.

"The easiest explanation." Christina chewed her lip as she looked out the window. Kai squeezed her hand.

"Looks nice," he told her.

"And not on a pleasure moon!"

"What's not on a pleasure moon?" Kimber asked.

Christina wouldn't answer, and Kai turned red.

"Are you talking about *popping the question?*" Auburn asked proudly.

"Dad!" Kai relaxed. They had a few minutes before landing. "She's worried I'm going to ask her to marry me while we're naked."

"What other way is there?" Auburn quipped.

Joseph shook his head.

Kimber buried her face in her hands.

"Did we forget about Terry and Char?" Christina tried to steer the conversation away from her. To anywhere other than her.

"No. We're trying not to think about them until we have more information," Cory added. "Ramses proposed by the shore of a lake after asking Dad for my hand."

"I remember that," Kimber said. "It took Dad a while to warm up to him, but you both won him over."

"We did." Cory smiled to herself as she ruffled Dokken's neck fur.

I will never understand human mating customs, Dokken told them. *I prefer our way.*

"Of course you do. You're a male." Kimber pointed an accusing finger at the German Shepherd and he sat straighter, proud of himself.

The Pod touched down, and the mirth evaporated. They rushed off with Christina in the lead. The others hurried to keep up as she stormed the front doors. The courteous staff opened them and bowed as she passed. She didn't acknowledge them as she headed straight for the counter.

"I'm Colonel Christina Lowell, and I am looking for Terry Henry and Charumati Walton."

The smiling green clerk from Torregidor waved over a supervisor, who asked the large group to follow her into a more private area.

The supervisor, also a green Torregidoran female, recounted everything that Christina had already been told, emphasizing the waiver and transfer of responsibility to the authorities on Cygnus VI.

Christina nodded politely, but as soon as the supervisor finished, Christina delivered her version.

"I don't give a flying goat-fuck about liability. We are

taking over in the search for Terry and Char. I guess I should say that we are beginning a formal search and rescue effort. I don't care about liability. We aren't out to give you bad press. We only want our people back. We have a heavy destroyer in orbit from which to conduct our search. Give us the details of their expedition, and we will take it from there."

The supervisor looked relieved. "They left seven days ago. Their room has been empty since, but it's paid for for one more night. I will escort you to the room so you can see if there is anything in their belongings that would help you.

Kimber and Cory jumped to their feet. Dokken was ready to go.

"Take them, and we'll stay here. I need to coordinate with my ship."

Christina and Kai remained behind while the others left with the supervisor. As soon as they were gone, Christina contacted the ship. *Micky, I need to know if any ships went anywhere near Okkoto in the past seven days. Smedley can hack the Cygnus VI security data if need be.*

No need at all, Micky said. *We've already pulled the information, as it is readily available to all Federation shipping. There is a standard flight path fairly close to Okkoto, but only ships accelerating away from Cygnus VI use it. No one slowed nearby, orbited, or descended to the surface of Okkoto besides the Venus recovery shuttle at exactly the forty-hour point after Terry and Char left.*

Then they have to be either there or here. Let me talk to the others. Christina waited for a moment to ensure that her comm chip was set for their group. *Talk to the shuttle pilot and crew. Turn this place upside down if you have to, but Kai and I are heading to Okkoto right now.*

They ran from the resort back to the Pod, and it took off while the ramp was lifting into place. "Straight to the ship, Smedley and set a course for Okkoto."

As soon as the drop ship entered the hangar bay, the *War Axe* accelerated at full combat speed toward the fourth moon. What had taken the resort shuttle an hour would take the *Axe* less than five minutes.

She leaned out of the shuttle. "I need four warriors in armor and four drop ships filled with search parties. Move, people!"

The Bad Company's Direct Action Branch had been waiting for word. They were still dogged from the action on Efluyez, but they had a job to do. The injured would survive. They were the only ones who weren't taking part in the search and rescue, not that they didn't want to.

Christina had told them no.

There was a minor argument about which warriors were going, and it was wasting time. Christina relented. "If you fit, you can come."

The warriors piled on board the drop ships, even those who had just come out of the Pod-docs.

Christina looked at the warrior who squeezed in next to her. "Didn't you die today?" she asked with the morbid humor that was prevalent in the Bad Company.

"Almost, ma'am, but not quite. Patched up and going back into battle."

"You don't remember getting blown up, do you?"

The man grinned. "Not a thing. I'm marching, and then

the door on the Pod-doc opens and I feel like a million credits. Better than a vacation!"

"You are one fucked-up dude," someone said, and the friendly back-and-forth shoving began.

"Launch," Micky broadcast.

The *War Axe* hit the outer atmosphere of Okkoto and the drop ships burst from the hangar bay, heading to four different points around the ancient ruins.

"Life signs," Smedley told them before Christina's drop ship landed. It maneuvered toward the signs and dropped the ramp.

She was first off, running in the direction Smedley indicated. It didn't take them long to find Terry and Char huddled in a crevice between two fallen walls. Christina tapped them on the shoulder, feeling how cold they were. She pulled Terry out first since he had wrapped his body around Char.

Two warriors tried to carry him, but he was too heavy. Two more joined them, and the four hustled toward the drop ship. Char managed to open her eyes.

"Come on. Time to go home." Christina and another warrior supported Char as they loped back to the ship. It took off as soon as they were aboard, and all four drop ships rocketed toward the *War Axe*.

Terry started shivering as soon as he warmed up enough for his body to regain control. The warriors wrapped both of them in blankets and gave them hot water from the small food processor on board.

"I have to say that you two have no idea how to take a vacation," Christina said.

"What do you mean?" Terry stammered. "Most relaxed I've been in years."

"In years," Char said, nuzzling into Terry's chest.

"Amateurs," Terry claimed.

Char snickered before dozing off in the comfort of the drop ship.

CHAPTER TWENTY-TWO

The *War Axe*

"You did fine," Terry reassured Christina and the company's senior leadership for the thousandth time. "I wouldn't have done as much in preparation, and we would have suffered worse for it. That's my highest compliment. It's good to be skeptical. Did we get paid?"

"Only the deposit," Smedley confirmed.

"Sonofabitch!" Christina exclaimed.

"Smedley, issue a reminder on that invoice and include the penalties for non-payment. Let's see if we have a treaty that needs to be signed."

The holoscreen over the captain's conference table shimmered to life, and the Magnate's secretary's face appeared.

"You!" Christina blurted.

"The Magnate cannot take your call right now, but I'm sure I can help you with whatever you need."

Terry motioned for calm. "No problem. Failure for the contract principal to reply activates our fifty percent kicker. You just earned us an extra quarter of a mil. Thank you." Smedley cut the line while the aide sputtered.

"He does that a lot," Christina clarified.

"Next order of business?" Terry asked. People were surprised by Terry and Char's immediate submersion back into managing the affairs of the Bad Company's Direct Action Branch.

"Call Bethany Anne?" Char suggested.

Terry was hesitant to call her without going through General Reynolds first, but he wanted answers, too.

"Smedley, connect us with High Tortuga, please. We'd like to talk with the Queen."

The system churned, and Smedley produced sound effects that represented old-style telephone calls with clicks and buzzes because it made Terry more comfortable. Ted was appalled by the failure to completely embrace new technology, but Smedley humored the boss.

Bethany Anne's eyes opened in a slight surprise. "TH! And there's Charumati and Christina! I haven't seen you in a while. To what do I owe the pleasure?"

"We wanted to thank you for saving our lives."

This time her eyebrows narrowed. "I have no idea what you are talking about, but I'm assuming I did something impressive. What did I do?"

Terry and Char looked at each other, surprised by BA's reply.

"We were trapped beneath the ruins on Okkoto in a place called Band Rayal Seven. They used Etheric energy to keep their shelter alive. You appeared while we were down there and fought some robots with us, and then you made it possible for the elevator to return us to the surface at the cost of your own life."

"The fuck?" BA's face went into full-on confusion. Looking down, she pinched her arm. "Pretty sure I didn't do anything lately that cost my life. Well, mostly lately." She looked to her right. "Michael?" she called to her husband off-screen before turning back to look into the monitor. "Nope. He confirms it. I'm still alive."

"But, you were there."

"As you wish." She shrugged. "Did you two perhaps get your heads smacked while you were out there?"

"I don't think so," Terry replied. "We'll have to go back to show you! There was an elevator."

"There was nothing in the ruins," Smedley answered.

"But..." Terry stopped speaking. Char looked at the table, searching her mind for a clue to support her reality. Terry looked equally out of touch.

There was some commotion off-screen that sounded like kids talking. "Gotta run. The twins are acting up." She winked at the screen. "Keep doing great things!"

The image faded.

Terry looked at the faces watching him. He wondered what they were thinking.

Micky stood. "I need to get back to the bridge." He clapped a hand on Terry's back. "Good to have you home, my friend."

"I need a beer," Terry said.

"Just so happens that Venus felt so bad about you paying for a room you didn't use, you were comped a rather significant amount of booze," Kimber explained.

"They felt bad because they abandoned us, but I may be

okay with that. Depends on the definition of 'significant.'" Terry cocked an eyebrow.

"We're going to have one hell of a party."

Char turned to Terry and shrugged. "It's what BA would want." She smiled.

"If she was here."

The End

Of Discovery, Book 6 of The Bad Company
If you like this book, please leave a review. Reviews buoy my spirits and stoke the fires of creativity.
Don't stop now! Keep turning the pages as Craig & Michael talk about their thoughts on this book and the overall project called the Age of Expansion (and if you haven't read the eleven-book prequel, the *Terry Henry Walton Chronicles*, now is a great time to take a look). Terry, Char, and the rest of the Bad Company's Direct Action Branch will return.

Welcome to the Age of Expansion

Written March 26th, 2019

I can't thank you enough for continuing to read this series. Terry Henry Walton and the fine characters who surround him have become a part of my world. I hope they've become a part of yours as well. Honor. Courage. Commitment. Something we can all live for and be proud of.

I went to the well once again, the Kurtherian Fans, and found Zayn Tova, offered by Lois Alston. That resonated for an Erthos character, so I went with it.

And our long-time USPS rural carrier found a new job, so that's Tonie. I told him I'd put him in a book so he would be memorialized forever, so here you have it—Tonie, digitally captured for as long as this book is in print.

I had to go to the foul-o-matic insult generator for some of the choice bits. One would think a Marine could be more creative, but alas, I needed a tactical assist from the computer, of all things.

And then I had to double-down and bring in the experts, the insider team of Jim Caplan, Micky Cocker, Kelly O'Donnell, and John Ashmore to further review and refine Bethany Anne's voice. Finally, I turned it over to Michael, who only changed most of BA's dialogue along with clearing up movement and places. He improved the flow, and here we are. Bob's your uncle.

I was having a minor issue with the sense of urgency within the plot, and that's when John Ashmore helped me solidify the idea of the Etheric crush. Thanks, John. That one tidbit helped to pull everything together.

This book delivers a standalone novel, something you can read if you've never read a single word of Terry or Char but are a fan of Bethany Anne. This book should speak to you. If it doesn't, then I have missed the mark. In any case, it gives you a little taste tempter of Bethany Anne while you're waiting for the next *Endgame*. I hope you stayed with us, and if you're reading this, you did. You read the book and the *Author Notes.*

That's it—break's over, back to writing the next book. Peace, fellow humans.

Please join my Newsletter (www.craigmartelle.com – please, please, please sign up!), or you can follow me on Facebook since you'll get the same opportunity to pick up some of the books at fan pricing (only 99 cents) on that first day they are published.

If you liked this story, you might like some of my other books. You can join my mailing list by dropping by my website **www.craigmartelle.com** or if you have any comments, shoot me a note at craig@craigmartelle.com. I am always happy to hear from people who've read my work. I try to answer every email I receive.

If you liked the story, please write a short review for me on Amazon. I greatly appreciate any kind words; even one or two sentences go a long way. The number of reviews an ebook receives greatly improves how well it does on Amazon.

Amazon – www.amazon.com/author/craigmartelle
Facebook – www.facebook.com/authorcraigmartelle
BookBub - https://www.bookbub.com/authors/craig-martelle
My web page – www.craigmartelle.com
Thank you for joining me on this incredible journey.

AUTHOR NOTES - MICHAEL ANDERLE

MAY 1, 2019

THANK YOU for not only reading this story but these *Author Notes* as well.

(I think I've been good with always opening with "thank you." If not, I need to edit the other *Author Notes*!)

BREAK's OVER, f<REDACTED>s!

So, I always find it odd when another author does Bethany Anne—not because of what they write, necessarily, but what it tells me they see in her.

For example, either Craig was channeling his inner Marine (which, frankly, is right next to his outer Marine) or BA is a bit of a hardass for hardassness' sake.

There were a few times that I realize I probably put these traits out there, but internally, I knew what her emotions were when she said something harsh to one of her people. Inside, she was doing it with care.

Outside for everyone else to see, she often comes across as a drill sergeant. Perhaps only a few who rarely interacted with BA assumed that her heart inside was warm and caring?

The caustic words often hide the worry Bethany Anne feels in her heart.

So, I got a chance to soften the words a bit, round out the effort BA made to get Terry Henry (who she thinks of as a cousin who just won't get his shit together) and Char.

Or was that just the BA that Terry Henry sees? Did the technology they were in create a version of BA which is inside Terry Henry and Char's minds?

Either way... She got the job done.

Because that is what Bethany Anne does.

AROUND THE WORLD IN 80 DAYS

One of the interesting (at least to me) aspects of my life is the ability to work from anywhere and at any time. In the future, I hope to re-read my own *Author Notes* and remember my life as a diary entry.

Cave in the Sky (™) Las Vegas, Nevada USA

I got told early this morning that I needed to have these author notes completed in twenty-four hours. I suppose I could have waited until tomorrow to write them, but even I think that might be cutting it kinda close.

It might also be that I am sort of hoping to sleep in late tomorrow since my first meeting is about 11:00 AM or so, and I want not to need to jump up early to get on any conference calls.

OR...

It might be that I'm ready to read all night and not stress with a job to do...

FAN PRICING

$0.99 Saturdays (new LMBPN stuff) and $0.99

Wednesday (both LMBPN books and friends of LMBPN books.) Get great stuff from us and others at tantalizing prices.

Go ahead. I bet you can't read just one.

Sign up here: http://lmbpn.com/email/.

HOW TO MARKET FOR BOOKS YOU LOVE

Review them so others have your thoughts, and tell friends and the dogs of your enemies (because who wants to talk to enemies?)... *Enough said ;-)*

Ad Aeternitatem,

Michael Anderle

Craig Martelle's other books (listed by series)

<u>Terry Henry Walton Chronicles</u> (co-written with Michael Anderle) – a post-apocalyptic paranormal adventure

<u>Gateway to the Universe</u> (co-written with Justin Sloan & Michael Anderle) – this book transitions the characters from the Terry Henry Walton Chronicles to The Bad Company

<u>The Bad Company</u> (co-written with Michael Anderle) – a military science fiction space opera

<u>End Times Alaska</u> (also available in audio) – a Permuted Press publication – a post-apocalyptic survivalist adventure

<u>The Free Trader</u> – a Young Adult Science Fiction Action Adventure

<u>Cygnus Space Opera</u> – A Young Adult Space Opera (set in the Free Trader universe)

<u>Darklanding</u> (co-written with Scott Moon) – a Space Western

<u>Rick Banik</u> – Spy & Terrorism Action Adventure

<u>Become a Successful Indie Author</u> – a non-fiction work

Enemy of my Enemy (co-written with Tim Marquitz) – a galactic alien military space opera

Superdreadnought (co-written with Tim Marquitz) – a military space opera

Metal Legion (co-written with Caleb Wachter) - a military space opera

End Days (co-written with E.E. Isherwood) – a post-apocalyptic adventure

Mystically Engineered (co-written with Valerie Emerson) – dragons in space

Monster Case Files (co-written with Kathryn Hearst) – a young-adult cozy mystery series

For a complete list of books from Craig, please see www. craigmartelle.com